CW01111834

HIS SECRET VIRGIN

A FORBIDDEN ROMANCE (THE SONS OF SIN SERIES BOOK THREE)

MICHELLE LOVE

HOT AND STEAMY ROMANCE

CONTENTS

Blurb	v
1. Chapter 1	1
2. Chapter 2	8
3. Chapter 3	14
4. Chapter 4	20
5. Chapter 5	27
6. Chapter 6	33
7. Chapter 7	40
8. Chapter 8	46
9. Chapter 9	53
10. Chapter 10	59
11. Chapter 11	66
12. Chapter 12	73
13. Chapter 13	79
14. Chapter 14	85
15. Chapter 15	92
16. Chapter 16	98
17. Chapter 17	105
18. Chapter 18	112
19. Chapter 19	119
20. Chapter 20	125
21. Chapter 21	131
22. Chpater 22	138
23. Chapter 23	144
24. Chapter 24	150
25. Chapter 25	156
26. Chapter 26	162
27. Chapter 27	168
28. Chapter 28	175
29. Chapter 29	181
30. Chapter 30	187
About the Author	195

Made in "The United States" by:

Michelle Love

© Copyright 2021

ISBN: 978-1-64808-855-1

ALL RIGHTS RESERVED. No part of this publication may be reproduced or transmitted in any form whatsoever, electronic, or mechanical, including photocopying, recording, or by any informational storage or retrieval system without express written, dated and signed permission from the author

❦ Created with Vellum

BLURB

Why did she have to be so young, so innocent, so damn sexy, and so forbidden...?

Done with relationships after a marriage rife with deceit, I knew I would never let myself fall in love again.
But then she walked through my door.
Barely twenty years old.
Shy as a kitten.
Innocent as a lamb.
And setting my body on fire for the first time in many, many years.
Her father and I were college buddies. She was his one and only child.
With everything in our way, it would be a miracle if ever get to feel her satin-smooth skin beneath my fingertips. To kiss those plump lips that begged for it. To taste her the way I knew no one else ever had.
If I did get my way, she would have to keep it all a secret. Would she be willing to do that for a man the same age as her father?

∼

Sexy, powerful, and twice my age; he took me by storm.

From the moment I saw him, I knew he was the one to show me a world I'd never experienced.
I didn't care that he was my father's age; maturity looked good on this man.
...And I couldn't shake the feeling that he was as attracted to me as I was to him.
He had an ex-wife who didn't want to let him go and a couple of daughters older than me that followed right along in their mother's footsteps.
...and my father was in my way.
With so much between us, would I ever get to feel him touch me in a way I'd never been touched in my twenty years? Would his mouth ever take mine in a savage kiss? Would my hips ever grind against his?
Would he be willing to fight with me for our love?

CHAPTER 1

Christopher

Not long ago, the laughter of my children always managed to stir my heart in a way nothing else ever had. Even as adults, the sound of their laughter riding the wind made me smile. When they were young, I lived my life for my girls. But time passed, life happened, and somehow that all changed.

My role as the doting father seemed like eons ago; now I had nothing, no one. And I couldn't be happier about it.

"Dad?" I heard my oldest, Lauren, call out. "We know you're home. Don't bother hiding from us. Ashley and I want to know all about how your forty-sixth birthday went yesterday."

My forty-sixth birthday. Fuck, I'm old!

Sitting on the back deck watching the sun as it dropped out of the sky, I didn't particularly want to hear anything my darling daughters had to say. They'd just come back from a weekend shopping spree with their bitch of a mother. I didn't want to hear a thing about my ex-wife.

Five blissful years of being happily divorced had gone by, and I looked forward to many more years of paradise without that banshee in my life.

"Dad?" Ashley called out in her sing-song voice. "Where are you? Come out, come out, wherever you are."

"On the deck, my loves." I figured I might as well let them say their piece and get it over with. The glass of Scotch I held in my hand would help steady me for their jabs, I hoped.

High heels clicked over the wooden floor as my always fashionable daughters made their way out to me. Lauren at twenty-five, had done little with her life thus far. It seemed she planned on majoring in purchasing all the clothing possible at the college of Daddy's Credit Card.

"There you are." Shuffling through her enormous purse, she fished out a yellow envelope. "From me, Daddy. Happy forty-sixth birthday." She punctuated her sentence with a kiss on my cheek.

"Thank you, my dear." Opening the envelope, I found a blue card inside. Fireworks covered the front of the card and exclaimed that I should have a happy one. Inside there was a signature, Lauren Taylor, and nothing more than that. "Well, it's only a day late." *And a dollar and sentiment short.* "Thank you, darling."

Ashley took a seat across from me then smoothed her hand over new denim jeans that fit her like a glove. "I didn't have a chance to get you a card." Her narrow shoulders moved with a shrug. "But you already have everything money can buy, so that makes it pretty hard to buy gifts for you."

"Sorry about that." I found it odd that my youngest daughter would try to make me feel guilty for not needing anything.

Ashley, at twenty-three, wasn't exactly a scholar either. Unfortunately, Lisa, their mother, never taught them much in terms of ambition. My ex's master plan was for our girls to do what she did: find a man, train him right, help him become a success, and then ride his coattails.

Lisa had done that for twenty-one years before I found out she'd been cheating on me throughout most of our marriage. I had been unhappy with our marriage for at least five years before I found her in our bed with another man.

Whether it was wrong of me or not, I was happy to have a legitimate reason to divorce the woman who'd made my life hell for what felt like an eternity.

Lauren took a seat at the table, grinning like the Cheshire Cat. "Mom said we should get you a cane for your birthday, old man."

I didn't find that so funny.

"I suppose it must be all the surgeries that made her forget she's a week older than me. But when you have to go in once a year to get your face lifted and every couple of years to get your fake boobs pulled up, I guess you forget how old you really are." I knew it was a shitty thing to say, but I didn't care.

"Put your claws away, Dad!" Ashley said with a smirk as she raked her hand in the air. "She told us to tell you happy birthday from her and that she would like nothing more than to join us some weekend, here at the lake."

It would be a cold day in Hell before I invited that woman to my home.

"Um, no." I took a sip of the Scotch to stop me from saying anything else.

I prided myself on keeping most of my unkind remarks to myself, trying not to vent to our daughters about their shitty mother. Today felt extra challenging.

When I left Lisa, I left her with the home we'd raised our children in. She could have that place. As far as I knew, she'd screwed men on every surface of that mansion. I wanted nothing to do with it.

Rushing to find a place of my own, I'd bought myself a small four-bedroom, five-bath home in Manchester. I had to stay in New Hampshire; my company demanded too much of my attention not to.

After the divorce was finalized and I was no longer afraid that Lisa would get half of everything I owned, I bought a large, stately mansion on the shores of Massabesic Lake, just outside of Manchester. Settling down in my own house, I was finally able to feel like myself again. It was my very own mansion, which I could furnish and decorate as I saw fit for once, and not how my wife dictated.

I wasn't in the new lake house long before Lauren came to me, asking if she could move in. Watching the unending parade of men through her mother's bedroom was getting old, even for her.

Not long after she moved in, Ashley showed up with her driver struggling to unload all of her things. "I'm moving in, Dad."

"I see that." With a nod, I'd let her move in; life returned to a bit of the routine I'd left behind when I moved out of our family home.

Having them in the house wasn't nearly as bad as it had been with their mother around to stir things up. The girls didn't bicker with each other as much as they had when we all lived under the same massive roof. They got along quite well, as a matter of fact. We all did.

Of course, I didn't try to make them do much of anything. They came and went as they pleased. Each had their own credit card that I would pay off each month.

They weren't completely spoiled. I did set limits on their cards. Only fifty thousand a month. If they met their limit, then they had nothing more to spend until the next month came around.

I thought it fair enough.

Somewhere deep inside I knew I should point my girls in some kind of direction. I wasn't getting any younger, and I wanted to make sure my girls could take care of themselves if anything should ever happen to me.

"I think you two should start thinking about college or a career or something."

"Why?" Ashley asked as she rolled her blue eyes. "We're just kidding about your age. You've got tons more time. No reason for us to get all worried about money right now."

Lauren smiled at me as she batted her long, dark, fake lashes. "Yeah, Daddy, why start worrying now?"

Taking another sip of Scotch, I wondered how I could possibly explain something as profound as doing a job, because you should be skilled in at least one thing in life. But nothing came to mind. "Okay, forget it."

"Even when you do kick it, we're set." Ashley reached out, taking the glass out of my hand. "You should stop drinking and maybe take up yoga so you'll live longer."

I took my glass back. "I don't need yoga when there's alcohol to help me relax after a tough day at work." Inspiration struck. "See, that's what I'm talking about. You girls should know how it feels to do a good day's work, to reap the rewards from doing that. It feels great to accomplish something. To set goals and to be able to see them through—it's more than satisfying."

"Um, no," Lauren spouted. "Mom says that we don't need to work. She says we're always going to have money. She made sure that you made tons of money, so she would never have to worry about it. And that money will continue to make more money until the day you die, and then it will still keep growing because of the investments you've made."

My God, these girls are spoiled rotten!

Pinching the bridge of my nose, I had to remind myself that I'd married their mother at the tender age of twenty. I'd been a dumb kid who'd fallen for the first female willing to suck my cock. Granted, she'd only done that while we dated. That shit went out the window as soon as my ring was on her finger.

So many things went out the window once I said 'I Do.'

The sweet way she'd say my name in her quiet, shy voice, "Christopher, come here, baby." That all changed. I was no longer her beloved Christopher; she'd started calling me Chris after our vows were said. Sweet names were no longer part of the marital package. And I didn't understand why.

After our graduation, Lisa began the daunting task of finding just the right job for me. I'd never thought about working in the food industry until she found an opening at a wholesale food company. I came in as a manager, and after I'd climbed the ladder to the top, she came to me with a new idea.

"Why not start your own company and take this one out of business?" she'd asked me one day. "I've made sure our credit is excellent.

You could get a business loan and start building up our company as soon as you want to, Chris. What do you say?"

I'd said yes. I did it all, just like she told me to. But I didn't make her my partner in any of it. *Thank God!*

She might've had the idea, but her involvement and interest in the company ended there. As long as I was bringing in money, she didn't care about anything else.

My divorce lawyer had been damn proud of me for leaving her out when I'd asked him to help me keep as much as I could with the divorce. Lisa had wanted half, and she wasn't budging on that.

Thanks to her infidelities, she got way less than half. I gave her our home, and she got to keep the three cars I'd paid for. In the end, all I had to provide her with was one billion dollars from my company, Global Distributing.

I counted myself lucky to have gotten away only losing that much. But I had to admit, she took much more than money from me. My ability to trust—to love—had crumbled along with my marriage. My desire to have a woman in my life was gone too. All I really wanted was to live happily ever after—alone.

Well, my girls could be around. But no romance was required, or even desired, in my life. Too many years of living with a self-serving narcissist had taken its toll on me. Love, lust, and even attraction were lost to me.

"Daddy, did you hear me?" Lauren asked.

I hadn't heard a word as I'd drifted off in my own thoughts. "No."

"I said that you should think about letting Mom come over for at least a cookout or something. You know how much she's always loved this lake. We could take her out on the boat. She'd love that. And she really wants to be your friend, Dad. She talked about you all weekend." She patted my hand. "Please."

I always had a hard time saying no to my girls—except when it came to their mother.

"No way in Hell, precious. I don't want your mother to come here. This is my place. One day, when you fall in love, you'll understand better. I don't hold any grudges or hate in my heart. That said, I don't want your mother involved in my life in any way."

Ashley swiped blonde locks so similar to her mother's out of her face. "See, I told you, Lauren. He can't get over what she did to him."

"Oh, I'm over it." I got up to go inside, needing to leave the whole conversation behind me. "And I want to stay over it. Night night, girls."

Aside from my daughters, women weren't something I wanted in my life, friend-wise or romance-wise.

I'm done!

CHAPTER 2

Emma

On my twentieth birthday, my dad had terrible news. Instead of coming home with the usual: a chocolate birthday cake and a bouquet of balloons, he came home empty handed. The look of despair on his face told me that there were more important things to worry about than a missing cake.

"Dad, are you okay?"

He shook his head and looked around the living room. "Where's Mom?"

"In the kitchen, cooking shrimp alfredo for my birthday dinner." I didn't like the way my father was acting. He'd never looked so bad. "What's wrong?"

Walking past me, he said, "Come on, I only want to say this once."

I followed him to the kitchen where my mother took one look at him and then dropped the spoon she'd been stirring with. She walked straight to him, hugging him tightly.

"Sebastien, what's happened?"

"The warehouse is shutting down." He sighed deeply. "The company went bankrupt. No one from corporate ever mentioned anything about any financial problems. I just got a call from the main office; I was told to tell my people that today is their last day, and that it's my last day too. Someone came from the bank to lock up the warehouse. It's been repossessed."

The shock made me feel numb. My father had been with that company since before I was born. I didn't understand how an entire company could just up and go out of business like that.

"I guess I should tell Laney at the boutique that I need to work full-time."

Mom let Dad out of the hug and looked at me with drooping eyes. "Yes, Emma, we'll all need to do whatever we can to make ends meet until your father can get another job."

"Celeste, you know I'm not going to find a job that'll pay me as well as the warehouse." Slumping over, he made it to a chair and sat down. Putting his head in his hands, he groaned. "I'm forty-six years old; no one's going to hire me."

"Well, that's ageism," my mother remarked. "I'm only a year younger than you, and I bet I can get a job. Besides, I'm sure there are a lot of managerial positions at any number of companies around here."

"Not one that pays what mine did." He lifted his eyes to look around the kitchen. "The mortgage payment alone will wipe out what's left in our bank account. Then there are the three car payments. The other bills will have to be paid too. I'm afraid we're going to lose everything, Celeste. You, Emma, and I can all go to work doing whatever we can, but it won't be as much as I've been making."

"You're talking like we're doomed, Sebastien." Mom went back to the stove to stir the sauce.

I jumped in to help her as I could see from her expression that Dad's words were weighing heavily on her despite her attempt at optimism.

"Here, Mom, let me help you."

Handing me the spoon, she went to the fridge and pulled out a beer. Popping the top, she placed it on the small kitchen table in front of my father. "Here, drink this. Hopefully, it'll settle your brain a bit. We'll figure things out, honey. I know we'll be fine."

After chugging the beer, a thing I'd never seen my father do, he put the empty can on the table. "Not the way we've been living, we won't."

"So, we downsize," Mom said with a positive attitude. "It won't kill us to trade our cars in for cheaper ones. Or better yet, we can trade all three in and just get one."

Dad looked like he wanted to cry. "I don't want you and Emma to lose your cars."

"I don't mind," I chimed in. "I'll do anything to help out, Dad."

He smiled, albeit weakly. "You're a good girl, Emma. My little baby girl."

"I'm kind of not a baby anymore, Dad. I did turn twenty today, you know," I reminded him.

"You'll always be my baby girl, Emma Hancock." Getting up, he hugged me and kissed the top of my head. "Happy birthday, sweetheart. I'm sorry I forgot to pick up the cake and balloons."

"There's no need to apologize. I understand completely." I kissed his cheek, which was bristly with a five o'clock shadow.

Letting me go, he went to the fridge and pulled out another beer. "I wish I could tell you that I'll make it up to you, but we're going to have to watch every penny until I figure something out."

After a solemn birthday dinner, I walked next door to visit my best friend, Valerie. She and I were the same age and had lived next door to each other forever.

She met me at the front door with a small pink bag in her hands. "Happy birthday, Emma!" She held it out to me. "I got you a little something."

I felt lucky that my birthday had fallen on a Friday. Otherwise, Emma would've been at her dorm at Columbia University in New York and not at home. "You didn't have to get me anything."

Placing the bag in my hands, she went on, "I know that. Just open it."

I pulled out a small box and opened the lid to find a charm for the bracelet she'd given me when I'd turned fifteen.

"An angel?" I looked at her for an explanation.

"Yes, I wanted you to have an angel to look over you." She ran her arm around my shoulders and then pulled me to walk with her to the back patio of her parents' house. "You see, Emma, I feel like you need some type of guardian in your life. You seem to be kind of stunted."

"Stunted?" I asked, feeling a little surprised by her words.

"Yes, stunted." She let go of my shoulders to take a seat at the patio table.

I sat down as well and then looked at the little angel with a sparkling clear crystal set in the middle of it. "This is very nice, Val. Thank you so much." I was trying to put an end to this conversation, wanting to move on from that awkward 'stunted' comment.

But she came right back to it. "Emma, what do you want to do with your life?"

And there it is.

"I work at the boutique, and I like doing that." I put the angel back into the box and back into the pink bag before placing it on the table, feeling a little prickly.

"Working at a boutique isn't a career, Emma." Her hands settled on her lap, psychiatrist style—not that Valerie took those types of classes at Columbia. She was majoring in English with the goal of becoming a teacher.

"And what does that mean, Valerie?" I knew what she meant; she meant that I should go to college too.

"It means that you need to broaden your horizons, and that means getting an education." Her dark eyes peered into mine. "If you don't want to go the traditional route, you can always get some type of certification. That never takes long."

"I don't have anything I want to get certified in." Then I thought about my father's job predicament. "Plus, Dad lost his job today. He can't pay for me to take any classes right now. I don't have any money saved, and even if I did, I would use it to help out my family."

She looked shocked. "Your dad lost his job?"

"Yeah." Fingering the fringe of my cut off denim shorts, I felt an odd sensation in the pit of my stomach. "I think there are a lot of changes ahead for my parents and me."

"I'm so sorry, Emma." She looked genuinely sorry, too. "If I would've known that, I wouldn't have brought this up. It's just that you're twenty now. A grownup. Not a kid anymore, you know?"

Valerie had always looked out for me. I knew she meant well, but she didn't understand me for a person who'd known me nearly my entire life.

"I know I'm not exactly a kid anymore. I just don't know what I really want to do with my life yet. I like where I work now. And Laney lets me help out, ordering the merchandise. I really like that part of the job. Besides, some people do work in retail their whole lives—and there's nothing wrong with that."

Slowly, she nodded. "Maybe you could be a buyer for a larger store like Macy's or something?"

She always did think big. But I've never cared about flash or grandeur. "I like the size of the store I'm working for now. You might not believe it, but making sure I pick out things that will sell in that small of a shop isn't exactly easy. The pressure of buying for a department store like Macy's would just be too much."

"Pressure isn't such a bad thing, Emma." She looked over the thick black frames of her glasses, giving me the teacher's expression she was starting to perfect. "Sometimes pressure helps build perfection."

"You just made that up, didn't you?" I laughed as she shrugged. "I knew it."

"All I'm saying is that pressure is inevitable in life. Stop running away from it and embrace it." She pushed the glasses back up on her nose. "I think that's why you've kept all the boys at a distance, too. You're afraid of the pressure they'd put on you if you let any who've made googly-eyes at you over the years do more than speak for two minutes."

Rolling my eyes, I had to correct her. "I give them all at least three minutes of my time, Val. You know that."

Shaking her head, she laughed, but she wasn't done with me. "A guy needs more than three minutes to get to know you—or you him for that matter."

"I haven't wanted to get to know any of the guys I've met like that. And I don't want any of them to get to know me." Besides, there was a bit more to it than that. I sighed. "First of all, you should know something—I haven't talked about it because frankly, it's embarrassing. I promised my father that I would let him talk to any guy I find myself interested in before ever going out on a date."

The look of pure confusion on her face told me that most girls didn't have the same problem I had. "Why would you make a promise like that, Emma? What is this, the 1950s? Are you insane?"

"No." But the way she looked at me had me rethinking that assessment. "Look, Dad knows me. He trusts me, and I trust him. And I do believe he has my best interests at heart."

"You're fooling yourself, girl." She leaned back in the chair, fanning herself. "You're a grown woman now, Emma Hancock. You're a beautiful young woman, too." She leaned up, propping her elbows on the table then her chin on her palms. "Maybe it's time you start embracing that. Hell, you're twenty, and I haven't even seen you wear makeup. Let me put some on you before you leave."

"Oh, no." I shook my head. "Dad would have a fit."

Rolling her eyes, she added, "I bet he would. But that doesn't mean you shouldn't wear it if you want to. Do it a little at a time and I bet he won't even notice it."

I knew he would. "No. Especially not right now. I've never seen him look as awful as he did when he came home today, Val. I mean it. I can't go shaking things up now."

Her lips pulled up to one side as she scrutinized me. "There will come a time when you will have to shake things up, little Emma Hancock."

Well, today will not be that day.

CHAPTER 3

Christopher

A soft rapping on my office door pulled my attention away from the computer screen. My assistant, Mrs. Kramer, opened the door, letting herself in.

"Mr. Taylor, how are you doing this morning?"

"Fine. I've received an interesting e-mail this morning. I may be on the next flight to China if the Skype meeting I'd like you to arrange works out." I turned the screen around for her to see. A handful of farmers wanted to grow organic crops, and they wanted my company to distribute them. Before I agreed to anything, I'd have to visit the farms myself. They would have to prove to me that their products were truly organic, or I wouldn't put them on my lists.

Sliding the tortoiseshell-framed reading glasses onto her thin face, she read the e-mail. "This is interesting." Turning my keyboard around, she tapped away on it, forwarding a copy to her e-mail. "I'll get on this meeting right away."

"Great." Sitting back, I put my hands behind my head. "A trip, even if it's just a quick business trip, will do me good. I've been in the office way too much the last few years."

"You have." She walked over to the coffee pot to make me some of her famous coffee. "But then again, you can't deny that focusing on work helped you forget about all the crap that was going on in your personal life. That's much better than turning to alcohol or something even more destructive, like so many people do when dealing with divorce."

"Well, there is that. But I probably drink a bit more than I should, too. I'm merely human." I thought about how different my life had been since leaving my wife. "But then again, I don't drink to drown my sorrows—I don't have any of those anymore. I do it because I can without anyone trying to make me feel guilty."

Not one to pry much into anyone's personal life, Mrs. Kramer quickly turned the conversation. "Mr. Taylor, I've been kind of falling behind on my work lately."

"I hadn't noticed." The woman never fell behind on anything. "Is everything okay?"

"Sure." She brushed her graying hair back after turning on the coffee machine. "It's just that you keep coming up with new projects so quickly that it's getting hard for me to keep up."

I had to remember that the woman was well past the age of retirement. But she had many good years left in her and wasn't the type to stay home and knit. "Should I slow down some?"

"No." She shook her head and then went to look out the window. "This company needs you to keep on doing what you've been doing." She turned to look at me again. "I love my job. I want to keep working until I can't anymore. With my husband gone now, being home doesn't feel the same."

Mrs. Kramer's husband had died two years earlier. The woman had handled herself professionally throughout the whole ordeal.

"I'm sure it doesn't feel the same." I nodded to her.

The coffee machine dinged as the brew filled the cup below it. She watched the dark liquid as it poured into the mug. "It never will." Her eyes cut to mine. "So, you see, I want to keep this job as long as you'll let me. I know a younger person could keep up with you a lot better, Mr. Taylor. But I'm going to need an assistant of my own if I'm going to be able to do it."

"Of course, you can have an assistant." I got up to grab the coffee, beating her to it. "Head to human resources and get them on it."

Her expression told me she felt relieved. "I was afraid you'd say you couldn't do that for me. It seems I've been worried for nothing."

It made me feel terrible that she'd think such a thing. "Mrs. Kramer, if you ever need anything at all, you just need to ask. I'm not trying to work you to death here. And I'm not trying to boot you out either. I want you to work here for as long as you want to. You're invaluable." It was the truth. "But don't forget, you've got a pretty great retirement here. If you feel like you need to stop working, then you do what's best. Life's too short not to live it the way you want to."

She nodded in agreement. "For now, I want to continue working. And getting an assistant will make things better—take some of the pressure off me." She made her way to the door. "I'll get to work on that meeting. It may take a day or so to get anything set with our time difference. I'll let you know as soon as I've got it all hashed out."

As she left, I thought about what it would be like when she wasn't my assistant anymore. Perhaps her new assistant might one day take her place.

I jotted a quick e-mail to her, telling her I wanted to be involved with the hiring of the new assistant. If that person could one day work for me, then I wanted to make sure I could get along with them too.

I'd become picky about the people I surrounded myself with since the divorce. Too many of my ex-wife's lovers were men I thought of as friends. And too many of the women that I thought were friends stopped talking to me in favor of maintaining a relationship with my ex. To be honest, I'd lost a bit of my faith in people as a whole.

Life hadn't turned out the way I thought it would. The relationship I put all my hopes and dreams into sank like the Titanic. My daughters had grown into shallow people. My friends were all but gone, as I'd cut them out one by one. Life wasn't going anywhere near the way I'd planned it.

Even though things hadn't worked out the way I'd thought they would, I wasn't sad, upset, or mad about it. I'd grown quite content with my life.

So what if my daughters were shallow? That was their life, not mine. I still loved them just the same.

So what if I made the mistake of marrying a woman who eventually cheated on me? It didn't ruin me. At least not completely. I still had my company; I still had my wealth.

And as far as cutting out the friends I'd had, I hadn't really lost anything. During my marriage, I'd surrounded myself with people just like Lisa. And who needs people around who are just trying to use you?

There wasn't anything for me to complain about. My company thrived. I spent my time spent wisely. And I had nothing or no one to worry about.

My daughters did make that part easy. Neither of them ever got into any trouble. No drugs. No partying like so many other rich kids. No promiscuous behavior. They could've been just like their mother, and that would've given me a reason to worry. But they didn't act like her in that regard. *Thank God!*

However, I knew if I ever tried to bring a woman around, there'd be trouble in my little slice of paradise. My daughters would turn into nasty little weasels then. I knew that for sure.

They weren't shy about telling me that it was their mother or no one for me. And not even their mother unless she turned over a new leaf.

Funny how they'd turned the tables on me. As their father, I should've been the one to give them hell about who they dated. But I stayed out of their love lives, preferring to remain ignorant on that score.

It might've been nice for the girls to butt out of my love life. But I didn't have one, so it never occurred to me to tell them off. And the fact that I had no desire to date made the idea of putting up a fight with my kids feel like an unnecessary chore.

Things were simple, and I adored simple.

Simple things always appealed to me. I liked Scotch neat, my favorite color was white, and hands down, I always prefer a peanut butter and strawberry jelly sandwich over any other food.

As I sat there thinking about what a simple man I was, a bit of anger began to seep in to me towards my ex-wife. She didn't have it bad with me. We rarely fought about anything. I let her have her way all the time. I gave her expensive gifts when she left hints about what she wanted. And I gave her everything and then some in our bedroom.

The slightest zing of pain shot through my heart.

With a sigh, I released the pain, letting it all go. "No reason to be hurt by what she did, old man. Selfish people only ever think of themselves. Don't take it personally." I'd made it through all the divorce ugliness by using those words.

Not taking things personally was the key for me. Those words had kept me sane for the last five years, and I had a firm belief that they'd continue providing me with peace of mind for years to come.

Another soft knock at my door, and Mrs. Kramer peeked her head in again. "Excuse me, Mr. Taylor. I wanted to ask you if you thought you could come back here around nine tonight for that Skype meeting? Mr. Wong and Mr. Lee will be available at nine in the morning, Beijing time."

"That's not a problem at all. Set it up." Getting out of my chair, I put on my jacket. "I'm going to go home and get some lunch. I'll take the rest of the day off then come back up here for the meeting."

"Since I'll have to be here for that meeting, too, may I also take the remainder of the day off, sir?" She looked at me with hope-filled eyes.

I had no idea how it had happened, but my assistant, the one who'd been with me from the very beginning, seemed to not know me at all. "Of course, you can take the rest of today off. I won't be here anyway. I'll see you at about eight-thirty then."

"Yes." She nodded then turned to leave. "Thank you, sir."

Reaching out, I put my hand on her shoulder, feeling like she needed a bit of reassurance. "Mrs. Kramer, you're a valued employee here at Global Distributing. I want you to know that."

"Thank you, sir." She looked at me with pale green eyes. "I've started worrying so much lately, wondering if the job I do could be done better by someone else, someone younger."

"Stop wondering. It can't be done better by anyone else." Patting her on the back, I hoped to make her feel more like herself. "Mrs. Kramer, not only are you a tremendous asset, you're a wonderful person, and I love having you as my right hand."

I thought I saw a glimmer of unshed tears in her eyes. "Thank you, Mr. Taylor. That's wonderful to hear. I don't know what's gotten into me lately. I just keep thinking about how I'm the oldest person working here and how I don't belong."

"You most definitely belong here, Mrs. Kramer. Please, never doubt that." Now I really felt bad about how much I'd been shutting people out of my life. "I know I've been distant for the last few years. I need to make some changes in myself. If I'm so closed off that I haven't noticed you feeling insecure, if I've been contributing to this issue of you feeling out of place, then I need to do something to change that. Thank you for opening my eyes. See you this evening."

Maybe my life did need to be punched up a bit, but how was I supposed to do that?

CHAPTER 4

Emma

Pink chiffon scarves littered the counter as I tagged them before putting them on display. Laney came out of the back with another box. "These were just delivered. I'm so happy they came in. These pink sunglasses will look so good displayed with those scarves you picked out."

"I think so too." I picked up a handful of the scarves. "I'll use that display stand over there since we'll be adding the sunglasses."

Laney put her hand on my shoulder to stop me. "Hang on a minute." Slipping a pair of sunglasses on me, she looked me over, and then took a scarf out of my hand to wrap it around my neck loosely. "Yes, you look great in pale pink. It goes so well with your golden-brown hair and green eyes." A smile curved her lips. "You keep these. And start wearing some of these clothes, Emma. You make them look great. It'll boost sales."

Ducking my head, I felt my cheeks heat with embarrassment. "I can't accept these."

"You can." Laney took the scarves from me. "I tell you what, go pick out an entire outfit to match the glasses and scarf. Then go put it on, and cut the tags off. I'm serious. I want you to wear the clothes I have on my racks, girl. You've got a great body, and you're so pretty too! I need to use that to get some sales."

Running my hand over my large hips, I had to disagree. "Laney, I don't have a great body. I've got a great *big* body." Looking in the full-length mirror, I shook my head at my reflection. "My butt is big—and not in a good way."

Laughter pealed through the air. "Your butt is fantastic, Emma. Go, pick out an outfit." I saw her fishing through a basket full of makeup. "And once you're all dressed, I'll do your makeup."

"My dad will get mad if I come home with makeup on, Laney." Saying it made me feel like a little kid, but it was true; he would get mad at me if I came home like that.

"Then you can wash it off before you leave." She put some of the things she'd found on the counter as she looked at me with a no-nonsense expression. "I'm not taking no for an answer."

Knowing she wouldn't let me get out of it, I turned away to find something to match the new accessories. I found a blouse with blues and purples and the slightest bit of pale pink. Pairing the shirt with a pair of billowy white slacks, I felt good about the outfit I picked out. "You like this, Laney?"

She shook her head. "Pick out something that will flatter your figure, not hide it. What you've got there is more for a woman with thirty extra pounds to hide." She eyed something across the boutique and went for it. "Like this."

After putting the clothes I'd picked back on their racks, I turned to find her holding up a top with a plunging neckline and a pale pink pencil skirt that would fit me like a glove.

"No way."

Cocking one brow, she laid down the law. "Yes way. Put them on. I'll grab a pair of heels to round this all out."

In the dressing room I pulled off the loose-fitting dress I'd worn to work. Staring at my reflection, I looked at my white cotton panties that covered my stomach to just below my belly button. My bra was on the bulky side to help hold up my big breasts. I hated my body. My tummy wasn't flat, but round like the rest of my body. Thick upper thighs turned into skinny calves and bony ankles. With a sigh, I put on the clothes I never would've chosen for myself and found that my panties and bra made the clothes look bulky; the outfit definitely didn't fit the way it would if I had something less unwieldy on underneath.

I went out to show Laney. "See, this won't work."

She looked me over as she walked toward me with a pair of four-inch lilac heels. "Not with that bra and underwear." Shaking her head, she walked over to the lingerie section and picked out a white satin set. "Put these on too. And do yourself a favor, Emma, throw all those granny panties out and those bras too. Invest in some cute unmentionables." She finished that off with a wink.

"I can't. Not right now, anyway." I took what she gave me then went back into the dressing room to start all over again.

With the right undergarments, it looked much nicer. "Wow, I look like I could work in an office or something."

"Wait until I do your hair and makeup." As the store wasn't busy at all, Laney set to work on me. It helped to fill our time, and Laney seemed thrilled with the results. "Wow, you look so different."

Just as she finished, one of our regulars came in and looked right at me. "Oh, hello," she said politely before looking at Laney. "You hired a new girl?"

Laney laughed then bumped her shoulder to mine. "See, you do look different."

"It's me, Mrs. Hampton." I couldn't believe she hadn't recognized me. "Emma."

"No!" she said as she looked me over. "Emma Hancock, I can't believe how great you look all dressed up and made up. You look so mature! You should keep this new look up."

Shrugging my shoulders, I knew that wasn't an option. "This makeup will have to go before I leave the boutique." I pointed at the low-cut shirt. "And this will have to come off, too, I'm afraid." Running my hand over my hip where the skirt hugged me tightly, I was sad to add it to the list of things that would have to come off before I went home. "This, too, unfortunately."

Laney gave me one ugly look. "No way, Emma. Tell your archaic father that I said it's part of your uniform for work. What can he say if you tell him that?"

I wasn't sure what he'd say. "Well, I do have to keep this job—he'll agree with that," I said with meaning.

Mrs. Hampton's expression turned to one of compassion. "I heard about the closure of his warehouse. That's tough. And there's not a lot for the workers to do around here. My nephew worked there as a loader. He packed up and moved all the way to Utah for a job. He's got some family there that he can stay with until he gets on his feet."

"Utah?" I asked. It hadn't occurred to me that my father might have to move somewhere else to find a job. "I hope Dad can find something here."

Shaking her head, Mrs. Hampton said, "It'll be tricky, that's for sure. He managed one of the biggest businesses in town. With the factory closed, there are more workers than jobs right now in our little city." She was right. Bristol, Rhode Island, didn't have a booming job market at the best of times.

"Yeah, he managed one of the biggest businesses in this town. So he should be able to get a job at one of the other large businesses here, right?"

Laney put her hand on my shoulder, looking sympathetic. "I don't know, Emma. Those other businesses have their own managers and people waiting in line to get those jobs. It might be tough for your dad—lots of companies around here hire from within. But I wish him all the best. And the fact that you have this job and you're switching to full-time will help. You'll be able to take care of yourself at least, and your parents won't have to support you."

Nodding, I knew she was right. "And Mom is looking for a job as we speak. You're right; all I have to do is tell Dad that if I want to keep this job, I have to adhere to your new dress code." It felt a little weird, but it seemed like forces beyond my control were pushing me out of my comfort zone. And I had to admit that I loved what I saw in the mirror.

Later, as I drove home, my tummy did flips as headed toward my house in the outfit Laney had given me. Just imagining my father's reaction kept me lightheaded. When I parked my car and headed inside, every step felt heavier than the last. "Come on, Emma, you can do this."

When I came in through the side door, I didn't hear anyone. "Mom? Dad?"

"Back here, honey," Dad called out.

Walking toward the den, I saw my parents sitting together on one of the sofas. The dim lighting hid me a bit as I came into the room.

"Hi, I'm home. Laney put me on full time today."

Dad squinted as he looked at me. "What the hell are you wearing?"

And here it goes.

My palms began to sweat. "Laney wants me to start wearing the clothes we sell at the store from now on. It makes sense, Dad."

Leaning over Mom, he flipped on the lamp beside her. "And what the hell is all over your face?"

"Makeup." My legs got shaky, and I had to take a seat before I fell; I was still wearing the heels, and while I'd gotten used to them throughout the day, my legs weren't up for this challenge. "Laney wants me to wear makeup while I'm at work. She'll do it for me there. I don't have to buy any or anything like that."

"And she did your hair too?" Mom asked.

I ran my hand through it, loving how silky it felt. "Yes, ma'am."

"It looks pretty," Mom said then looked at my father. "She looks nice, Sebastien."

With a huff, he put in his two cents, "She looks like she's thirty years old."

"I don't think so," I said in a whisper.

"You do." He looked down at the floor then back up at me. "Emma, there's no need to rush growing up. Now go on and wash that crap off your face. And those clothes aren't appropriate. I understand your boss wants you to wear them at work, but I'd prefer if you changed into your own clothes before you come home. Hopefully, you won't have that job much longer anyway."

That was news to me. "What do you mean by that? Don't you need me to keep this job, Dad?"

"Right now, I do. But I'm going to make a phone call to an old friend of mine." He reached over to pick up the can of beer that sat on the table in front of him. "Christopher Taylor has a very successful business, and I hope he might have a place for me in his company."

"I've never heard of him." I chewed my lower lip as butterflies began to take flight in my stomach. "He's not from around here, is he?"

"No, he's not." Dad put the beer back on the table. "His company is in Manchester, New Hampshire."

I'd never been to New Hampshire. "How far is that from here?"

"About two and a half hours. That's if traffic is good. Which it usually isn't." He picked up his beer again and took a drink.

Mom took over. "If your father can get a job there, then we'd sell this house and move closer."

"To Manchester?" I asked in disbelief.

We'd always lived right where we were, here in our home in Bristol. I didn't want to leave, to have to start all over in an unfamiliar place.

"Yes, we would move to Manchester, Emma. I think a change of scenery would be nice. Don't you?" Mom smiled really big to entice me to join her in the spirit of change.

It didn't work. "No. Mom, I don't want to move. I've got Valerie here. She's like my only real friend. And my job. I love my job."

"Valerie goes to Columbia in New York," Mom reminded me. "She can drive to Manchester to see you. And there are jobs there too. This would be a great opportunity for your father if it all works out. Global Distributing is one of the largest food distribution companies in the world."

Dad nodded. "So, go on and change out of those clothes. And hopefully, I'll know if I've got a job or not by tomorrow. If I do, you can quit that job, and then you won't have to wear makeup or inappropriate clothing."

"But you should still do your hair like that, Emma," Mom said. "It looks nice that way."

"I just took it out of the ponytail and Laney ran over it with a hair straightener." I walked away with my shoulders slumped. "I suppose I can learn to do it myself. But I was hoping she could teach me how to do my makeup."

"You don't need to know how to do that," Dad called out after me. "You're just fine without it, honey."

"But I'm better with it," I mumbled underneath my breath.

Crossing my fingers, I silently hoped Dad's friend wouldn't have a job for him.

Soon after, I uncrossed them and changed my negative thought to a positive one, hoping for the very best for all of us. And hoping that the very best thing would be what I wanted, which was to stay right where we were.

CHAPTER 5

Christopher

"Sounds great, Mr. Lee." The Skype meeting had been successful, and the men had been able to show me enough of their operations to prove the quality of their organic crops right then and there. No trip to China would be necessary, but they wanted to come meet me sometime in the near future and tour our facility. "We'll set up a trip for you two soon."

Mrs. Kramer wrapped up the session as I walked out the door to head back home. I'd turned my cell on silent for the meeting. Taking it out of my pocket, I saw I'd missed a call from an old friend from my college days.

It had been many years since I'd seen Sebastien Hancock. The call piqued my curiosity, making me wonder what he could possibly be calling about. Meeting my driver outside, I got into the backseat and called Sebastien back right away.

"Hey there, old buddy."

His tone was happy as he said, "Christopher, glad you called me back."

"Of course. It's nice to hear a friendly voice." I couldn't even count the number of years that had passed since we'd seen each other. "What's it been, five years? Ten? How's Celeste doing?"

"She's doing fine. As beautiful as ever." He sighed. "I'm one lucky son of a bitch, and I know it. And how's Lisa doing?"

Well, this conversation was off to an awkward start. "We divorced five years ago when I found out she was cheating on me every chance she got."

"Shit." Sebastien sounded shocked. "I'm sorry to hear that. Did you guys have any more kids? How are the girls doing? They must be pretty grown up now."

"No, just the two girls. They're twenty-five and twenty-three now." I watched as my driver pulled into the garage and saw that neither of the girls' cars was there. "They live with me now, but they're hardly ever home. And did you and Celeste have a brood of kids?"

"Not hardly." He chuckled. "We've just got our one daughter. She just turned twenty and is trying to act thirty if you know what I mean."

"Oh yeah, I do." I knew he called for more than a little catch up, so I cut to the chase. "So, what has you calling your old friend, Sebastien?"

"I suppose it's best to get right to the point and not skirt around this." I heard him take a drink of something, maybe to work up his courage. "I lost my job. The entire company just went belly up. It was a shock to me and everyone who worked under me. I'm looking for a job, buddy. I'll take whatever you can give me."

My heart went out to the guy. I'd seen many companies close in my time. That's precisely why I worked as hard as I did to keep mine in business. "What were you doing at that company?"

"Managing the warehouse," he answered. "Getting paid really well for it, too, after giving them my life for the last twenty or so years."

"That is tough, Sebastien." I thought about what I could offer him. He'd been a great friend back in our college days, and I didn't want to let him down. "With that experience, I'm sure you could be a great help to me."

"Glad to hear that," he sounded relieved. "I'm a fast learner, so anything you've got, I can learn."

"I'm sure you could." I had a couple of guys I could move around to fit my old buddy in. "Tell you what, how about I get my human resources department to give you a call tomorrow morning, about nine or ten. I'll talk to them and see what we can offer you. Will you be able to relocate here?"

"I can. We can put our house on the market, and my family can stay here until it sells. I'll stay in a motel until then." His voice went a lot quieter as he continued, "It'll be the first time I've been away from them for any length of time, but they'll be okay."

The thought of him having to separate from his family didn't sit right with me. "Is your daughter still living at home too? Hasn't she gone off to college? Maybe your wife could come to stay in a motel with you if your daughter's away at school."

"That's not the case. Emma is still living at home. I don't mind though; I like having her close." I heard him take another drink before saying, "I'll just have to do what I have to do is all."

Maybe because my earlier conversation with Mrs. Kramer was still lingering in my brain, but I suddenly found myself putting forth an uncharacteristic offer. "I've got a house you can stay in. I bought a small home when I left my wife. Nothing too fancy, five bedrooms, six baths, only a four-car garage, but it does have a pool in the back and a hot tub too. I left all the furnishings in it, too, once I bought my new place on the lake. You're all welcome to stay in it."

"That would be awesome!" His excitement was obvious. "What do you want for rent?"

"Rent?" I couldn't charge him anything. "No, there won't be any rent. Hell, if you like the home, you can buy it from me directly, and we can take the payments out of your check. But until you decide, you'll be my guest. I'll have my staff go over there and make sure it's all cleaned—make sure the yard's taken care of and the pool is up and ready to use too."

Now that the offer was out there, I felt great about it. The fact my old friend would be around made me lighthearted and happier than

I'd been in a very long time. I'd been avoiding people for much too long. Maybe this was the beginning of a change for me. Perhaps I could make room for at least one close friend in my life.

"Christopher, that's more than generous. I'm sure your HR department and I can come to an agreement on the job and the money. And let me tell you that my family will be over the moon with this news." He seemed very happy, and that made me happy.

"I can't wait to see you and Celeste again. And meeting your daughter will be nice too." I thought about my girls. "You said she's twenty, right?"

"Yeah, she's twenty," he said. "But she's really shy."

"My girls can pull her out of her shell. They've got lots of friends. I'll ask them to take her around and introduce her to everyone." I hoped my girls would be nice to his daughter and take her under their wings.

"That won't be necessary, Christopher," he said, sounding a little grumpy. "We're pretty strict with her, so she doesn't go out much. No makeup, no boys, no parties while she's under my roof. But it's nice of you to offer."

A twenty year old who hasn't gone on a date?

I felt sorry for her already. Hopefully she was having at least a little fun behind her father's back—what he didn't know couldn't hurt him. "Well, maybe things will be different up here. Manchester isn't a dangerous place. And my girls have never gotten into any trouble. I'm sure your daughter could use a friend or two here while you all settle in. I would hate for her to be unhappy living in Manchester."

Hesitantly, he said, "We'll see. I'm looking forward to hearing from your company tomorrow, Christopher. I really appreciate this, you know. Now I get to tell the wife and kid the great news."

"I'm glad I could help, Sebastien. And I'm glad you'll be around. It's been a long time since I've spent time with friends; I'm really looking forward to you moving here and working at my company." I really was, too. For the first time in a long time, I was looking forward to something.

"I'm looking forward to it as well." He waited a second then went on, "I don't suppose you would have anything for my daughter to do at the company, too, would you?"

With no idea of what the girl was like or what she could do, I wasn't sure about her. "Does she have a job now?"

"She works in a boutique, selling clothes, makeup, stuff like that," he told me.

"Well, we don't have a need for anyone to do that kind of work here." I thought about it for a moment then added, "But I'm sure we can find something for her to do here. What are her career goals?"

"She's a kid, Christopher; she has no career goals yet," he said with a laugh.

He left me with little to work with. "I suppose you should bring her in with you when you come to fill out all the paperwork. I'll feel her out and see where she might work out, and where she'd be happy working." I hated to put people in positions they didn't like.

With her background in retail and customer service, I might even be able to put her into the sales department, but I wouldn't know until I met her. It sounded like my friend kept her on a very short leash. I wondered how much he would even allow her to do.

"Well, maybe she'll develop some goals by working here," I added. I had hopes that we could help the young woman blossom.

I knew I hadn't been able to do that with my girls, as I'd let their mother do the raising of them. Thanks to her, I hadn't been allowed much influence there.

According to Lisa, my only role as father was to provide, and I did that very well. Maybe my friend's daughter would allow me to help her find something that would fulfill her. It would be nice to mentor a young person since I couldn't do that for my own daughters.

"Emma will do fine, I'm sure," Sebastien said. "I'll talk to you tomorrow. Have a great night and thank you so much. Goodbye."

Stepping out of the car that the driver had parked in the garage, I went in through the side door to the kitchen. The cook had left out a peanut butter and jelly sandwich for me, just as I'd asked her to.

Feeling happy about what the future might hold for me, I picked up the food and took a bite. A glass of milk would go perfectly with it, so I went to pour myself some.

I took my food and drink to the table and sat down. I'd never paid attention to how empty the house felt. The staff had all gone home for the night. Sitting in my empty house, I felt alone for the first time in a very long time.

It would be nice to have a friend again. Someone to invite over for barbeques and other fun stuff—that would certainly be a change for me.

A very good change.

CHAPTER 6

Emma

The new job offer was great news for Dad, but it wasn't all that great for me. His friend had come through for him big time. Dad landed the job as the manager of Chinese produce, a new division that Mr. Taylor had just started.

Along with the new job came a house that bordered on being a mansion compared to the house I grew up in. Five bedrooms, six baths, four living areas, three dining areas, and a pool with a built-in hot tub; our new home was more than I could've ever dreamed of.

The four-car garage left one space empty, and Dad quickly proclaimed that he would be buying a motorcycle to fill that space. Mr. Taylor paid Dad a salary that was twice as much as what he had been making at his old company. My father had never been happier in his entire life, and he told us that all the time.

Not long after we arrived at our new home, Dad told me to get myself ready for an interview. He and Mr. Taylor had talked about me working at the company, but Mr. Taylor wanted to meet me—to feel me out to see where I would fit best.

I'd never been more nervous. The new company car sped along as

Dad drove me to the giant building that housed the offices of Global Distributing.

"This place is huge," I gushed as I got out of my father's car.

"It's a monster, isn't it?" He glowed as he walked up the steps with me right on his heels.

I wasn't rushing alongside him because of excitement, but for fear I'd get lost if I didn't keep up. "There're so many people here. I can't believe he even needs either of us."

"Well, luckily, he does." Dad pushed the elevator button, and we stepped into the packed lift when it arrived. I could smell that someone had just had coffee for breakfast; another person smelled like donuts. I focused on the people around me to avoid thinking about the scrutiny that I would soon face from Mr. Taylor.

We went all the way to the top, and only one other person was left to get off with us. The man was wearing a suit and tie, and looked like a real professional. Dad did, too, wearing a new suit and tie. I was the only one who looked like I wouldn't fit in.

My blue dress went all the way down to my ankles, and I wore flats. My hair was pulled back into a ponytail, a matching silk ribbon wrapped around it. My father had helped me pick out my outfit. He said it made me look my age. I thought it made me look six years old.

My heart pounded as I followed my dad to Mr. Taylor's office. "It's just at the end of this hallway. I've got an office up here too." He pointed to a door that had his name on a gold nameplate about halfway down the long corridor.

"Wow, Dad. Cool," I gushed. "Can I see your office when this is over?"

"You bet." He stopped at Mr. Taylor's door. I took a deep breath, trying to tell myself that it was no big deal that the man who sat behind that door held my future in his hands. "Here we are."

After Dad knocked, a deep voice called out, "Come in, Sebastien."

"Wow, how'd he know it was you?" I asked.

"Surveillance cameras." He pointed at the tiny camera above the door we stood in front of.

"Oh, yeah." I felt a little stupid for not noticing it before.

As my dad opened the door, my eyes were immediately drawn to the tall man who stood by a counter with an expensive coffee machine on it. He turned to us with a cup of steaming liquid in his hand. "You made it, Sebastien. And this must be Emma."

I couldn't think, much less talk. But Dad bumped me with his shoulder. "Shake his hand, Emma."

Only then did I notice Mr. Taylor's extended hand. "Oh, sorry. Hi, Mr. Taylor. My father's told me a lot about you." I almost blurted something about his divorce—my dad had filled me in about that on our drive over—and that would've been super inappropriate. "It's nice to meet you."

"Sir," Dad whispered.

"Sir," I added.

"It's a pleasure to meet you, too, Emma Hancock," his voice was smooth, rich, deep, and sophisticated. It took my breath away.

But it was the touch of his hand that set off feelings that I'd never experienced before. My core felt hot. My panties felt damp. Something inside me vibrated.

When I looked up into his eyes—eyes that were a stunning combination of green and brown all mixed up in the most fantastic way—my heart stopped. "Hi." I felt starstruck even though the man wasn't a star.

He laughed lightly then kept hold of my hand, pulling me to a chair. "Here, take a seat." After I sat down, he held out the cup of coffee to me. "Care for some coffee, Emma?"

"Emma doesn't drink coffee, Christopher," Dad told him.

My cheeks blazed with embarrassment. I'd never wanted anything more in my life than for this man to look at me like a woman and not like the little kid my dad wished I could still be. I wanted to be all woman to this man, and I had no idea why.

Mr. Taylor looked at my father for a second before drinking the coffee himself. "Well, let's see. How to go about this," he paused for a moment, but quickly continued. "Emma, tell me what kinds of things you like to do. Hobbies, special interests, anything like that." He leaned back on his desk.

The length of his legs made my mouth water, and I didn't understand that reaction at all. Thick as tree trunks, I could see his thighs were all muscle. The suit he wore did little to hide the fact that his arms were massive as well.

"Do you work out?" I asked him, instead of answering his question.

"Emma!" Dad snarled.

I dropped my head. "Sorry."

"That's okay, Sebastien," Mr. Taylor said. "I do work out. Is that something you like to do as well?"

"I never have." I looked up at him. "But I think I would like it." *Especially if I could work out with you.*

Something was wrong with me. I wasn't thinking straight. I definitely wasn't talking straight either.

I caught my father pinching the bridge of his nose. "Emma, try to concentrate, honey. Tell Mr. Taylor what kinds of things you think you might be able to help with at the office."

"I can type really fast." I tried not to look directly at the man. He stirred me in such a way that it made it hard to think or breathe. "I'm a fast learner. I can do just about anything asked of me."

"That's good," he said. He moved around to sit behind his desk.

I looked him over as his back was to me. He kept his dark hair short and parted on one side. It made him look both masculine and dashing at the same time. I'd never thought of anyone as dashing, but that's the exact word that came to mind as I thought about Mr. Taylor.

"I can also clean pretty well, too, Mr. Taylor." The way his name slipped off my tongue felt good. And I noticed his eyes jump a bit when he turned to look at me before sitting down.

"I'm not going to put you into the janitorial department, Emma. I'm leaning toward making you an assistant." He placed the cup of coffee on his desk then steepled his long, thick fingers, touching the tips of them together, making me wonder what the tips of his fingers might feel like as they ran over my skin.

Hiding my hands by my sides, I crossed my fingers for luck. *Please make me your assistant!*

"I would love that, sir." I tried to think of other things that would make me a good assistant. "I don't drink coffee, but I know how to make it. And I know how to answer phones too. I could answer your phone for you."

"Not mine," he said with a laugh. "My assistant has been with me for years. She makes my coffee. And I tend to answer my own phone calls. I'm not talking about you becoming my assistant, if that's what you were thinking."

Damn!

"Oh, I could be anyone's assistant, sir." I hoped that helped make me look a little less stupid to the man.

He and my father were the same age. Yet he looked so different. So agile. So sexy.

"Do you drive, Emma?" he asked as he opened a file he'd pulled from the top drawer of his desk.

"I do, sir." I had to put my hands in my lap to hold them still. They'd begun to shake.

Why does this man have to be the first man to turn me on like this?
Why does he have to be my father's friend?
Why does he have to be my father's age?
What the hell is wrong with me?

I'd never gotten flustered with any guy my age. And I knew some good-looking guys. Sure, I hadn't talked to any of them that much, but I knew them.

So, why did this man have such an effect on me?

When he looked up, his eyes danced a bit as he looked into mine. "My assistant needs an assistant. That would involve some driving. She picks up my laundry and delivers it to my home, but that would become your job. And she scouts places for me from time to time."

"Scouts?" I had to ask.

Dad came up behind me. "That means she goes to look at places for him to judge if they're good for what he needs them for. And I think Emma could do that."

Mr. Taylor looked at Dad. "I'm sure she can." He got up, going over to my father. "I think I can handle it all from here, Sebastien. I'll get her all set up. My assistant will want to talk to her and then we'll get her to human resources to get all her paperwork signed. And she'll be issued a company car, too, so you don't have to wait around for her today."

Dad looked over his shoulder at me as Mr. Taylor led him out of the office—a thing I was both happy and afraid for. "Looks like you've got a job, honey. Make Daddy proud."

"She's not in kindergarten, Sebastien," Mr. Taylor said quietly, but I heard him anyway as his deep voice traveled. "Try to let her spread her wings."

"You're right." I'd never heard my dad admit that anyone was right when it came to me. In his opinion, he—and he alone—knew what was best for me. "See you later, Christopher. And thanks for this."

"You're welcome. I'll see you at lunch. I've got a few things I want to talk about with you, and we can do it over lunch," Mr. Taylor said before closing the door, leaving us all alone in his office.

My blood went from scorching hot to ice cold. *I'm alone with Mr. Taylor!*

He walked back to sit behind his desk. "Normally, I don't hire people just because a relative works here. But your father is a very dear friend. I hope it won't offend you when I try to advise him to stop babying you when I see him doing it."

"No, sir." I was happy he'd said something to my father. "I understand."

"Good. I want us to be one big happy family here." Leaning forward, he smiled, and I nearly passed out—it was that brilliant. "I've got a couple of daughters who aren't that much older than you, Emma. What do you think about meeting them sometime?"

"Oh, I don't know." My hands twisted in my lap. "I'm sure they're so... so cool and sophisticated like you are. I wouldn't fit in with them. I know I wouldn't. But that's very nice of you to ask."

His expression turned to one of concern. "Emma, may I ask you something a little personal?" He waited for my nod and then continued. "Did you choose your own outfit today? Was it your own choice today not to wear makeup for this interview?"

"Dad doesn't allow it, and he suggested the outfit," I said much too quickly. "But I think the makeup thing is so that my face never breaks out. He said he had lots of trouble with acne when he was a teenager, and he never wanted me to have to go through that."

"Admirable," Mr. Taylor mused. "But you're not a teen anymore, and I think a little makeup wouldn't hurt your skin at all. But I should say that you've got remarkably smooth skin. My daughters would be envious. If you don't mind one old man's advice, I'd say maybe just a bit of blush, some lipstick, and a little eye makeup would make you look more your age. Right now you resemble a twelve-year-old—no offense intended."

My cheeks went red, and my head dropped. "I agree."

The next thing I felt was his hand on my chin, pulling my face up. "No reason to be embarrassed, Emma. So, what do you say? Would you like to be my assistant's assistant?"

"I would, sir. I would love that."

And I would love it if you never removed your hand from my face!

CHAPTER 7

Christopher

Touching her made things stir in me that hadn't rustled in years. My hand lingered, fingers barely touching her chin, as sparks radiated throughout my body.

"Good, Emma. I think we'll work well together." The urge to draw her lips to mine had me pulling my hand away as if burned.

I'd never been so tempted in my life. Her golden-brown hair, pulled back into a sophomoric ponytail and tied with a blue satin ribbon, looked ridiculous on a girl her age. I yearned to pull it out to let her hair fall down her back. I imagined she'd have beautiful loose waves when it was unrestrained.

Her dark green eyes looked like translucent pools on a forest floor. I could drown a happy man in those pools.

What am I thinking?

Not only was she my friend's beloved daughter, but a girl younger than my own daughters. What a crime that this girl was the first to make my dick hard since my ex-wife had over twenty years ago.

"I think we'll work well together, too, Mr. Taylor." She licked her pink lips as her eyes cut to the floor.

She needed to gain some self esteem, and I knew I could instill that in her. I needed to think of her as a young person, and not a grown woman who attracted me more than I knew was possible.

"First things first then." I went back to take a seat behind my desk so as to hide my arousal and to make myself feel more like her employer and less like some old dude with a hard-on. "Mrs. Kramer will talk to you about appropriate office attire, and I want you to make sure you listen. You'll be issued a company credit card for all the expenses that pertain to your job here. And that means getting clothes, shoes, makeup, etcetera, to make yourself look the part of an administrator's assistant. That's your job title, by the way."

Her pretty face lit up like a bottle rocket. "I get a credit card and a company car all on my first day?"

"You do." I loved the way she'd perked up so quickly. And then my damn eyes went to her breasts that had perked up with the rest of her as she sat up straight.

Damn my eyes!

Why do her tits have to be so damn perfect?

Why is her ass so round and pert?

Does her waist have to be just the right size for my hands to wrap around, moving her up and down as she...

Stop it!

The fabric stretching across my engorging male member became uncomfortable to say the least. It took all I had to write down what I wanted Mrs. Kramer to do for Emma. But I got it done.

"This is like a dream come true." She laughed lightly, and the sound made my heart thump hard in my chest. "Although I must say I never dreamt about an opportunity quite like this one. I guess I just never dared to dream this big. And Dad told me that you're letting us live in your home—and what a beautiful home it is!" Her eyes sparkled, holding my attention as she gushed. "It's like a mansion to us. We've never stayed in anything so... um...grand?"

If she liked that place, she'd love my lake house. "I'll be sure to have you all over for dinner sometime soon, and you can see my lake house."

"That would be so cool!" The way her face radiated with excitement turned me on even further.

So not right!

"Yes, so cool," I mumbled. I wanted to close my eyes for a moment to distract myself, but I knew that would come across as weird and probably even creepy. I took a deep breath instead and thought about baseball statistics. "Anyway, let's get you all set up. You'll have the office next to my assistant's."

Her eyes went wide as she looked thoroughly surprised. "No way! My own office too?" She looked out the window. "Is it up here on the top floor?"

"It is." I couldn't help but smile at how excited she was. Never in all my years had I hired someone who got such a kick out of the little things. "You'll have your own desk and computer and even a private bathroom."

"No way," she whispered. "I can't believe you're doing all this for me. How can I thank you properly?"

Well, you could come on over here and bend over my desk for me.

I shook off that thought. "Just do a good job, and that will suffice, Emma."

With a sigh, she said, "I'll give it my best shot. You'll get one hundred percent from me, sir. I promise you that."

Inappropriate thoughts flooded my brain. I had to stop them before I did something totally unprofessional—and totally out of character. "I can see that you'll work out well here." Pushing the buzzer to summon Mrs. Kramer, I steadied myself to make sure she didn't get any hint that I was quickly becoming enamored with young Emma.

After a swift knock, my assistant came in, her eyes trained on Emma. "Hello, I'm Mrs. Kramer. And what can I do for you, Mr. Taylor?"

"Well, you can ask Emma Hancock any questions you have as she's your new assistant," I told her.

She cocked one brow. "You've hired her already?"

"I did." I supposed I'd aggravated her some by doing the hiring without her, and without her getting to even meet Emma beforehand. "She's on a trial basis until we see which department she'll be the happiest and most productive in. I wanted her under the very best tutelage, and that would mean working under you, Mrs. Kramer."

Her ruffled feathers were smoothed with my words. "Oh well, of course. I would love to take her under my wing and show her how this company runs."

"Good. She's the daughter of that old friend of mine that I've just hired, Sebastien Hancock." I pushed the notes I'd jotted down to the edge of the desk. "And I know this isn't the usual protocol, but I want her to be issued these things. And please help her with appropriate office attire, please."

Emma sat up, placing her hands on her knees as she looked at Mrs. Kramer. "I do have a very good idea of what to wear when working here. The trouble isn't my fashion sense, exactly; it's more my father's approval and his idea of what is and isn't appropriate."

The way Mrs. Kramer looked at her told me she wasn't sure about Emma. "How old are you, young lady?"

"Twenty," Emma said with a certain amount of pride.

"Then you're plenty old enough to wear what you want." Mrs. Kramer took the note I'd written and placed it into the pocket of her skirt. "Office attire is the exact opposite of clothing that people would find offensive. If your father finds that the things I suggest for you are inappropriate, then he and I can have a discussion about it. You leave him to me, dear."

Sitting back, Emma nodded her head cautiously. "I can't say my father is going to be a fan of this, but thank you very much for helping me."

I could see she was feeling a little nervous. "Don't worry about your father, Emma. Mrs. Kramer and I are always professional when it comes to this company. I can promise you that neither of us will make your father uncomfortable. And may I say that I really admire that about you."

"Admire what about me?" she asked with a puzzled expression.

"The way you care about your father's feelings." I had a feeling that beneath the child-like exterior, this one had a wealth of caring and loyalty beyond her years.

My brain abruptly took that moment to reminded me that her father had said he'd never let her date. And that fact led me to make some other assumptions about this young woman—she was probably still a virgin. My imagination grasped onto that thought and went a step further, thinking that she might never have been kissed either. And then my cock went and thought that she had very likely never experienced an orgasm, and all it wanted to do was help her out with that.

"Can I take her with me then, Mr. Taylor?" Mrs. Kramer asked, pulling me out of my sexual stupor.

"Yes!" my word came out a bit too enthusiastically, earning me an odd look from my assistant.

"Very well then." She turned to look at Emma. "If you will follow me, we'll get you all squared away. Today will be all about paperwork and issuing you everything you'll need to be my assistant. Tomorrow we'll get down to training you. By the end of the week, I think you'll be all on your own. Won't that be nice?"

Emma got up, following Mrs. Kramer out of my office. "That sounds great."

My eyes were glued to her plump ass as it shifted back and forth underneath the loose-fitting dress. Closing my eyes, I said, "See you girls later, then."

Emma's voice had my eyes opening again as she said, "Thank you so much for this opportunity, Mr. Taylor. I promise that I won't disappoint you."

"I'm sure you won't." Uncharacteristically, I waved at her. "Have a good first day, Emma Hancock."

Mrs. Kramer let Emma walk out first and stopped just before closing the door. "I would like it if you called her Miss Hancock, sir."

"Okay then, Mrs. Kramer." I wondered if she'd picked up on my attraction, and that possibility embarrassed me a little.

"Thank you, sir." She closed the door, leaving me alone with my terrible thoughts.

Placing my head in my hands, I had no idea what had just happened. A girl walked into my office with her father, dressed like an overgrown child, and my libido went off the charts.

Something had to be wrong with me. Maybe it had just been way too long since I'd had sex with a woman. Perhaps I'd have the same reaction to the next pretty face I came across.

I decided to see if that was indeed the case and got up to leave my office. As I strolled down the long hallway, my erection finally eased off, leaving me feeling much more comfortable.

When I got to the elevator to head down to the main floor, a very good-looking, age-appropriate woman stepped off of it. "Good morning, Mr. Taylor."

I had no idea who she was. "Hello. Good morning to you, too." My cock paid no attention to her at all.

"You don't remember me, do you?" she asked.

Shaking my head, I admitted, "No, I don't. Should I?"

"I temped up here last month." She pointed at the reception desk. "Over there. You passed me each morning, and we said hello?"

"Oh, yes. Of course." I didn't recall her at all. But it'd be rude to tell her that. "Nice to see you again. Are you temping up here for someone else today?"

"No, sir. I had an appointment with Mrs. Kramer, your admin. She asked me to come up and interview with her about a position as her assistant." She smiled brightly. "It would be a pleasure to get to work so closely with you both."

Scratching my chin, I wondered how to tell her that that wouldn't be happening. "I should give you a heads up. I've already hired someone just this morning. Mrs. Kramer had no idea. But please keep your appointment with her, so she doesn't think you skipped it."

Looking a little deflated, her smile faded. "Oh, I see."

"I'm sure you'll find something else," I offered before stepping onto the elevator to head downstairs.

She hadn't piqued my interest at all. I hoped someone would—and soon—so I could forget about little Miss Emma Hancock.

CHAPTER 8

Emma

Driving home in my new company car, a brand new Ford Fusion in dark blue, I listened to the radio and thought about how much my life had just changed.

The day progressed swiftly, and I had felt a bit overwhelmed by everything. This could be the start of a real career for me—what if I ended up spending my whole life working at Global Distributing?

Working with Mrs. Kramer had gone well, though—the woman couldn't have been nicer. But she had seemed a bit surprised by all the things Mr. Taylor had given me.

I couldn't say that I was all that surprised. He and my father were good friends, after all. Mr. Taylor had proven to be a very generous man.

Pulling into the drive, I decided to park in the garage in the space occupied by my current car. That one could be parked outside and maybe even sold sometime soon. After all, why would I need to drive it anymore?

Jumping out to move my old Chevy, I ran around until I got everything situated. Just as I pulled the company car in, a delivery truck pulled up. Surprisingly, the clothing items Mrs. Kramer had helped me order online were already being delivered.

Hurrying out to meet the delivery man, I greeted him cheerily, "Hi!"

"Well, hello there, miss." He opened up the large back door then took out three boxes. "These are for a Miss Hancock. Does that happen to be you?"

"It does." Giddiness took over as I thought about all the new clothes I could add to my closet.

"Can you sign this for me?" He held out a clipboard with an invoice on it.

I signed the bottom and then dug in my purse to give the older man a tip. "Here you go, sir."

He shook his head. "No need. Your boss took care of that. Mr. Taylor gave me a generous tip when he came by to make sure the clothes would be delivered today."

"He did?" I had no idea he'd done such a nice thing. "That was nice of him."

"Yes, it was," he agreed.

I couldn't help but wonder why Mr. Taylor would go to all that trouble for me. But then I thought about how I'd dressed that day, and how helpful he had been in dealing with my father. It started to make a bit more sense to me; he wanted to help me become more independent, and getting clothing I actually liked was the first step. Taking the boxes, I thanked the man and went inside, marching straight up to my bedroom.

After trying on each and every item, I put them all away and then laid out the outfit I'd chosen for the next day. Mom opened the door, looking with surprise at my now-filled closet. "And what's all this, Emma?"

"Mrs. Kramer, the woman I've been hired to assist, helped me pick out all these clothes." I pointed at the clothes lying on the bed. "I'm wearing this tomorrow."

"Your father told me you'd been given a company car," she said. "Were you given an expense account too?"

I pulled the credit card out of my purse. "I got my own credit card to help with anything I'll need for my job—clothes included. Mrs. Kramer said my limit each month is five thousand dollars. Can you believe that?"

"No." She took the card out of my hand. "Let me see that."

"It works," I said. "I used it to purchase all this online. Mr. Taylor stopped by the actual department store downtown to make sure they got delivered today. He's so nice, Mom."

"I know he is. I met him when he was one of your Dad's groomsmen at our wedding." Mom handed the card back to me. "So, he's been very generous with you, I see."

"I bet if you want a job there, he'll give you one too." I thought about how cool it would be if we all worked at the same place.

She didn't seem to like that idea much. "Dad and I spend enough time together. It's best to have a bit of distance in a healthy relationship. Think about that while you're working, Emma. Dating someone you work with can get very hairy. It's not something I recommend."

I rolled my eyes. "As if Dad would even let me date, Mom."

"Honey," she wrapped her arm around my shoulders, pressing her head to mine, "you're twenty now. Do you know what that means?"

"Not really." I pulled away from her so I could look at her. "What does that mean, Mom?"

"Your father hasn't told you this yet," she whispered as if he was somewhere near when in fact he hadn't come home from work yet, "so don't tell him I told you this."

Curiosity compelled me to ask, "Tell me what, Mom?"

She winked at me. "That your father has decided that he doesn't need to meet any young man you want to date before you can go out now. But again, I must tell you that dating someone you work with is just a terrible idea. I cannot stress that enough."

I had no idea my dad had been planning on lifting his archaic rule. And I also had no idea who I would even want to date. What I did know was that Mr. Taylor immediately flashed in my mind.

"Well, there's no one to date yet. Maybe I'll meet someone, somehow, outside of work." I didn't know how that would happen, as I had no friends yet and had never made friends quickly. But maybe things would be different here in Manchester.

Things already felt different. I had to admit that I'd never felt the way I had when Mr. Taylor talked to me. The shyness that usually prevented me from getting to know people had all but disappeared when I spoke with him. And Mrs. Kramer made me feel okay, too. She was sweet and so much older that I hadn't initially put her in the same league as one would put a friend.

But in what league did I put Mr. Taylor?

"There's a pretty cute young man who delivered the newspaper today," Mom said as she wiggled her eyebrows at me.

"A paperboy, Mom?" I wiggled mine right back at her. "Come on. I think I can do better than that."

How about the owner of a multinational company?

Who was I kidding? Christopher Taylor would never be interested in me.

Mom walked toward the door. "Dinner will be ready in an hour. It's Swedish meatballs. And your father called to tell me that Saturday evening we'll be going to Christopher's lake house for dinner. He's set on introducing you to his daughters, I think."

My stomach twisted. "No! I don't want to meet them. I know we won't have anything in common."

Mom stopped at the door, turning to look at me. "Emma, I'm sure you three will have something in common. You're all around the same age. If nothing else, you can talk about music. All of you kids like the same stuff in that area."

I was really getting tired of my parents treating me like a child. I wasn't some kid who needed her mommy and daddy to arrange a playdate with the other kids. "Mom, I don't want to go, so count me out." I wouldn't be pushed into meeting anyone I didn't feel comfortable with.

With a *tsk*, she let me know how my father would feel about that, "Emma, you know your dad will make you go."

I did know that he would try. "I'll talk to him. Sometimes I can get him to see my side of things. Mom, it'll make me look so...*losery*."

"I do not believe that losery is a word, Emma." With a huff, she blew her hair out of her face. "I know you didn't like school, but you were taught to use better grammar than that, young lady."

"Well, you do get what I'm saying." Sitting at the end of my bed, I thought of a better way to word it. "I'll come off as a loser who has to use her parents to meet other people my own age. And, by the way, I don't generally get along with girls my own age."

She rolled her eyes. "Emma, you're not eighty. I know you don't like to do all the stuff most girls like, but I think that might be because your father never allowed you to. Maybe you and I should go get our nails done. We could even get facials and haircuts from a fancy salon. Heck, maybe I'll even get some highlights put in my hair; I'm feeling adventurous. What do you think about that? A new look to go with your new clothes and new job?"

I couldn't deny that I found the idea very tempting. "Sure, Mom. Set it all up. Don't forget my work schedule, though. Nine to five, Monday to Friday. I get an hour for lunch, but I don't think that's enough time to do any of those things."

"No, it's not." She put her finger on her lower lip, the way she always did when she was thinking about something. "How about we do it Saturday morning? That way we'll be all done before we head out to Christopher's for dinner. You can meet his daughters as the new and improved Emma Hancock. It's time your father allowed you a bit more freedom to grow."

I would be shocked if he'd okayed any of this. "Okay, Mom. You set it all up, and I'll do it."

"Great." She clapped her hands with a smile and then left me alone.

My father would have to do a heck of a lot of changing if he'd allow all that. And I knew he hadn't done much changing at all. Twentieth birthday or not, Dad still saw me as his little girl.

As far as I knew, Mom had never questioned Dad about any of his decisions where I was concerned. He ran the family. She ran the house. And I did what they both told me. I didn't see any of that changing.

My cell lit up, and I saw Valerie's name on it. "Hi, Val. You'll never believe how fantastic my day has been!"

"Tell me, girl!" she shrieked.

"Well, first off, I've got a new job. Assistant to the main man's assistant," I gushed.

"Wow," she sounded a little surprised. "I have to be honest, I thought you'd start out in the mailroom. But you've got a nice title there, Emma. Good going."

"It gets better." I lay on my bed, looking up at the ceiling. "I've got my own office on the top floor with all the bigwigs. And I have a company car. It's a brand new Ford Focus in dark blue."

"No way," came her envious reaction. "I can't believe it."

"There's more." I sat up as excitement filled me. "I've got a company credit card with a limit of five thousand dollars a month, which I can use to buy anything work related—like clothes to wear to work. Shoes. Makeup. Everything!"

Silence met my ears, and then she screamed, "Oh my God! I can't believe it. My little friend sounds like she's finally going to grow up."

I thought about what Mr. Taylor said about not letting Dad baby me. "You know, I think my father really respects our boss, Mr. Taylor. He's his friend from college—remember I told you all about him?"

"Yeah. That's good that your dad respects him. It sounds like Mr. Taylor respects your dad, too, since he's given you this cushy job and all the perks that go with it."

"Yeah well, Mr. Taylor told me that he's going to be making sure my father starts treating me more like an adult." I fell back on my bed again as I thought about the man. "He's so gorgeous, Val. Like totally hot."

"Wait, what?" she asked. "Hold on. This guy and your dad went to school together, Emma. He's an old man. You can't possibly think he's hot."

"I bet if you Google him—Christopher Taylor, owner of Global

Distributing—you'll find pictures of him." I dared her to think any differently than I did.

"Okay, let me do just that." I heard her tapping away on the laptop she always had around. "Okay, Christopher Taylor, owner of—oh, shit! He is hot!"

Thought so.

CHAPTER 9

Christopher

As I left my office to head to the café downstairs for a mid-morning snack, I saw Emma leaving Mrs. Kramer's office, looking as if she had an errand to run. "How's your first real day going, Emma?"

She looked up, seeming stunned to see me. "Um, it's going okay. Mrs. Kramer sent me to get us something to snack on. She said there's a café just around the corner and she wants a fruit cup with extra pineapple."

"I'm heading there too." I couldn't help the thrill that ran through me that she and I could legitimately hang out for a little while. "I'm not sure what I want yet. Yollie has specials each day, but she never gives a hint what they might be beforehand. I usually try out whatever she's serving up."

She nodded. "I'm sure I'll find something I'll like. I'm not even hungry, but Mrs. Kramer said that it's better to eat small portions throughout the day to keep up one's energy levels than it is to eat only three large meals."

"She got that from me," I let her know. "When I got divorced, I started working out, and a nutritionist at my gym put me on the right path. With all the unhappiness in my marriage, I'd developed terrible eating habits, and I was consuming way too much alcohol, too. But a person has to cope somehow."

She looked pained a bit. "I'm so sorry your marriage went so badly, sir."

I couldn't believe I'd even mentioned my marriage to her. I didn't talk to anyone about that horrible part of my life. "I shouldn't have said anything." I tried to change the topic, "So, are you missing your friends from back home yet?"

"No." She shrugged. "Val is my only real friend. She's going to Columbia, just like you and Dad did. She was very impressed with me for landing this job, and I know I only got it because of my dad, but I'm very excited about it, too, Mr. Taylor."

"Good," I found myself putting my hand on her shoulder to steer her toward the elevator. And there was that sensation again, like lightning crackling through my veins. I almost asked her if she could feel it, too, as she looked up at me with a funny expression on her face. Then I noticed she'd put on the tiniest amount of makeup. "I see you're wearing some mascara and a little blush today. It looks nice. Did your dad say anything to you about it?"

"He hasn't seen me yet." She watched the doors of the elevator as they closed, shutting us off from the rest of the people in the building. I'd led her to my private elevator; no one would be getting on with us. I wasn't even sure why I'd done such a thing. "Um, no one else got on. Usually the elevators are packed."

"This one is private." I looked at her outfit approvingly then realized my hand still rested on her shoulder. Moving it, I commented on her clothing choice. "Nice suit. The black slacks fit you perfectly, the pale green blouse accents your eyes very nicely, and the string of pearls adds just the right touch."

She smiled as she kicked out one low-heeled black shoe. "And the shoes bring it all together, right?"

"They do." I found her so sweet that my mouth watered. "Did your dad give you any trouble over the new clothing?"

"Well, I didn't tell him about that either. He left the house before me this morning." She looked down at the floor. "I thought it best for him to see me first at work and maybe then he wouldn't put up a fuss."

Taking her chin in my hand, I lifted her face. "Emma, just a word of advice. Don't drop your head so much. It makes you look timid. You have no reason to be timid. Not around here, you don't."

"I suppose you're right." She smiled at me with brilliant white teeth that gleamed. They made her even prettier. "I've just always been shy. I've always tried to blend into the woodwork."

"Well, you're not in the town you grew up in," I reminded her. "You get to start fresh here. No one will think worse of you if you hold your head high, keep your shoulders back, and look people in the eyes. You get to reinvent yourself here, Miss Hancock." I suddenly remembered that Mrs. Kramer had asked me to call Emma by her last name.

She giggled. "You don't have to call me that, Mr. Taylor."

The elevator stopped on the ground floor. "Oh, but I do. You're an up and coming administrative assistant. Everyone will call you Miss Hancock. Why should I be any different?"

Her smile made my heart speed up. To see her that way just did things to me. I couldn't explain it if I tried.

With the lobby so busy, no one noticed that she and I walked out the door together. Once outside, I walked along beside her. She glanced sideways at me. "Would it bother you if I didn't come with my parents to dinner at your lake house on Saturday night?"

It would actually.

I didn't say that though. "How come you don't want to come?"

She shrugged her narrow shoulders. "I don't know how to explain it very well. I just don't want your daughters to see me as some weirdo who has to make friends with people just because their parents know each other."

"That makes sense." I stopped at the small café. "Here we are." Opening the door, I let her walk in first.

"Good, so you understand then?" she asked as she walked past me. The scent of her hair wafted past my nose.

"Um, honeysuckles," I muttered.

She looked back at me. "Pardon? I didn't quite hear you."

"Nothing." Putting my hand on the small of her back, I walked with her up to the front. "Look, the special today is my all-time favorite."

"Oh, mine too." She leaned forward to ask, "Is the jelly on the sandwich strawberry?"

My heart shouldn't have swelled over that, but I couldn't stop it.

Yollie answered with her usual boisterous voice, "Is there any other kind?"

"Not in my opinion," Emma answered. "Can I have one of those and a fruit cup with extra pineapple, please?"

"I'll take the special, too, Yollie." I looked down at Emma as she stood beside me. "I think a glass of milk would be good too. How about you?"

"I do think that would be good." She looked at Yollie. "Can I have a glass as well?"

"Sure thing," Yollie said as she went to work making our snack.

"Put it all on my tab, Yollie," I called out and then took Emma by the elbow, steering her to a small table for two. "We can eat right here."

She looked a little wary. "Will Mrs. Kramer be okay with that?"

"Tell her you met me here, and I insisted you eat with me." I couldn't help but smile. "She won't give you any trouble if you say that."

"I bet you're right." Taking the seat right across from mine, I noticed how close our knees were to touching. I swear I could feel the electricity sparking between us.

"I guess I can forgive you for not coming to my place on Saturday." I had really wanted her to come, but I understood why she didn't want to. "The fact is, my daughters may not even be there. And another fact is that they're nothing like you. They've never worked a day in their lives and don't plan to. They may not understand why you're working at all. I don't want them to make you feel bad about yourself."

"Thank you, sir." She started to drop her head then stopped herself halfway. Her eyes came up to meet mine, practicing what I'd just talked to her about. "I don't know that we'd have much common ground between us, since they come from such a wealthy family. But I understand why they don't work. They just don't need to. And taking the place of someone who really needs that income would be selfish. But that's just my opinion."

I'd never considered it that way. "You know something, Emma—I mean Miss Hancock—I've never thought about it that way."

She reached across the table, putting her hand on top of mine. "Really, I don't think you need to call me that outside the office. Do you?" She moved her hand away from mine, leaving my skin tingling.

My cock began an ascent as my heart raced. Swallowing hard, I said, "If you'd rather me not call you that outside the office, I won't."

"It's just that you and Dad are such good friends. It's inevitable that we'll be around each other outside of work, and that would feel weird, you calling me Miss Hancock." She ran her hand through her hair.

"Well, then how about this," I knew I was treading on thin ice, "How about you call me Christopher when we're outside of the office? You know, since we'll be around each other more than most bosses and employees?"

Her pretty green eyes went wide. "Um, I don't know if Dad will let me do that."

"I'll tell him that I insist." I decided to add, "And I don't think it's his decision to make. But if he gives you grief, I'll tell him it's because my daughters never call anyone by their last names. That's a habit they learned from their mother. She raised them, for the most part. My job was to bring home the bacon, and hers was to rear the children. Old-fashioned, I know. That's just the way it was in our marriage, sham that it was." And there I was again, talking about my marriage. "Sorry."

"About what?" She looked clueless.

"I don't need to be talking about my marriage with you—you probably don't want to hear anything about it." I looked at the counter as Yollie put our order on it. "I'll get that for us." Jumping up, I went to grab our food.

"Let me," she said as she tried to get up.

I put my hands on her little shoulders. "No. I'll get it, Emma."

Every touch fired my blood, and I knew it was all wrong. *How can I keep my distance from her?*

As I went to get the food, I wondered if I should start seeing a shrink or something. What I felt wasn't right at all.

"Thanks, Yollie." I picked up the tray as she eyed me with a little smirk. "What?"

"You have never, in all these years, eaten with anyone here, Mr. Taylor." She jerked her head toward Emma. "So, who exactly is she?"

"She's one of my friend's daughters, and she's working for me now. She doesn't know anyone in town or at the company yet, and we just happened to meet up on the way out to grab a snack before lunch." I didn't know why I felt the need to explain everything to her, but there I was, explaining it all.

I have to nip these feelings in the bud before I do something that could destroy my friendship with Sebastien.

CHAPTER 10

Emma

The whole first week of work, Mr. Taylor and I ate our daily snack together. We somehow ended up going at the same time each day, running into each other every day. And I always loved the special Yollie made. Although the PB&J had been my favorite.

When Saturday came, I faked a stomachache, and Dad let me stay home. But he did tell me that I would have to go the next time Christopher invited us. Dad wasn't of the same mind as his friend when it came to my explanation of why I didn't want to be forced to meet Christopher's daughters.

That didn't surprise me much. But one way my father did surprise me—quite pleasantly, I might add—was when he told me how great I looked in my business attire and how much he approved of the new look. The tiny bit of makeup I'd been wearing was okay by him. Most of my skin was still makeup-free. I didn't use foundation, just a little bit of brown mascara, pink blush, and pink lip stain.

I'd grown to love it so much, I don't think I would've stopped even if he hadn't approved.

At the end of the first week, everything seemed to be going well.

But then Monday rolled around. When I set out to get our mid-morning snack, Mr. Taylor was nowhere to be seen. Tuesday came, and the same thing happened. Wednesday had my shoulders sagging as there was still no sign of him.

Has he grown bored with our daily conversations?

I couldn't help but think that he had to be avoiding me. Maybe he felt the tension between us, too—which I thought might be sexual. Perhaps he didn't feel it, and only I did. Maybe I had imagined it all. Or more likely, he'd only been being nice to me for my father's sake.

Little by little as each day passed, I began to think I'd been a fool for ever believing that a man my father's age would actually be attracted to me.

Walking alone to Yollie's café, I thought back on my past encounters with him. The way it felt like pure fire running through my veins every time Christopher touched me. The way his hazel eyes lit up when he saw me in the corridor. The way his voice changed and got deeper once we were sitting alone together in the café.

Sure, I didn't know a thing about romance, love, sex. Even so, my body seemed to be running on instinct. It felt hot when he came close. It cooled when we parted ways. And my mind stayed on Mr. Christopher Taylor all day long—and all night, too.

I picked out clothes to impress him. I put my hair in styles I thought he might like. I wore perfumes and washed my hair and body with the scent of honeysuckles because I'd heard him murmur that word when I walked past him that first day in the café.

Everything I could think to do to entice him, I did. And then he went and hid from me the very next week.

Val told me I'd been crazy to think a grown man like him would ever want to be with me. Not that I wasn't a catch, but he had people to impress. A twenty-year-old on a playboy's arm is one thing, she'd said. A twenty-year-old on a billionaire business tycoon's arm is quite another.

Deep down, I knew she was right about everything, but it didn't sting any less.

When Thursday came, I'd lost all hope that I'd ever get the chance to feel Mr. Taylor's beautiful hands roam over my entire body.

I might've been inexperienced when it came to sex—hell, I'd never even had an orgasm—but that didn't mean I didn't have those urges. The truth was, no matter how heated my thoughts about Christopher Taylor became in the middle of the night, I fretted about giving myself that ultimate pleasure. I worried that I might scream like a wildcat when I came for the first time. If my parents heard that, I would most likely die of embarrassment.

So all I was left with were my thoughts and daydreams, and as the days passed without any contact with Mr. Taylor, even those were tinged by a feeling of hopelessness.

The end of the workday on Thursday came, and I felt like a deflated balloon. With only one more day left in the work week, I pretty much knew I would not so much as set my eyes on the gorgeous, and now elusive, Christopher Taylor.

Walking out to the parking garage, I saw my father just ahead of me. "Hey Dad, you leaving too?"

He stopped, turning to look at me. "Hey there, honey. You look kind of blue. Rough day?"

It hadn't been rough at all. Mrs. Kramer made sure her game always ran smooth. "Nah. Maybe I'm just a little tired. I'm still getting used to this schedule."

"Yeah," Dad put his arm around me, and I rested my head on his shoulder. "Your old job at the boutique doesn't even compare to this one, does it? But I've got to tell you that I'm the proudest I've ever been of you, sweetie."

"You are?" I raised my head to look him in the eyes to make sure he'd told me the truth. I couldn't remember Dad ever telling me he was proud of me.

"Of course," he said with a genuine smile. "Emma, you jumped in to help your family when you shouldn't have had to. I thought we'd be just about broke right now. And now that I'm able to cover all the bills again, you've got yourself a nice little salary of your own. And I'm very proud of the way you've been conducted yourself at the office; I've only been hearing glowing reviews."

"Dad." I put my head back on his shoulder, giving him a hug and squeezing him tight. "You're the best dad ever."

"Aw, hearing that never gets old." He kissed the top of my head, making me feel a little bit better than I had been earlier.

"Sebastien, wait up," I heard a deep voice coming from behind us.

Christopher!

I jerked my head off Dad's shoulder and looked back to see I'd been right. But the man wasn't looking at me. His eyes were focused on my dad.

Dad stopped and turned us to face his friend. "Hey, Christopher, what's up?"

Jogging up to us, a brief waft of the scent of his intoxicating, manly perspiration made my heart palpitate. I didn't know if that was good or bad. Or maybe I just had an irregular heartbeat and might need to get to a hospital or something.

Wiping his dark brow, Christopher looked smoking hot in workout clothes. His chiseled muscles were on perfect display!

His shorts let me see his tight, toned, rigidly muscular legs. A white T-shirt, soaked with his sweat, had become nearly see-through as it clung to his pecs and abs. A trickle of sweat moved down the side of his thick neck, and I nearly passed out as I followed its trail with my eyes. How glad I was that Dad still had his arm around me so I could lean on him.

"What's up is that I'm going to need you to step in for Brad from the Vermont sector. He's out all of next week. His wife just had a baby. You know how that goes." Christopher didn't even acknowledge me.

I felt more than a little incensed. I mean a 'hello' would've sufficed. I would've been over the moon with just that.

"I'm not up on the Vermont stuff, but I can read up on it." Dad let me go, and I nearly fell over, jumping around a bit to catch myself. "Oh, sorry, sweetie. I didn't realize you were leaning on me so much."

I ran my hand over my hot face, hoping there was no blush that would give my heated thoughts away. "That's okay. I'll get going and leave you two to your conversation. It sounds important."

"Nonsense," Dad said. "Wait a sec."

Never one to challenge my father in public, I waited. My skin felt like it might be on fire, and my head throbbed in a way I didn't understand at all. To top it all off, my eyes kept on moving all over Christopher's body as my nose quivered, urging me to just lean in and take a long deep whiff of him.

Christopher went on, "I'm going to need you to go to Vermont this weekend. You can take Celeste. Hell, make a romantic weekend out of it. You'll be visiting an apple orchard and a vineyard too. Have fun. All I need are lots of pictures. And the company will cover it all, of course. You can't beat that now, can you?"

Dad looked at me with a frown. "Can Emma come too?"

Christopher's expression went south, and he lowered his voice as if I wouldn't be able to hear him. "Why would you want your daughter to come with you and your wife on a romantic weekend, buddy?"

With a shrug, Dad answered, " 'Cause I don't like to leave her home all alone."

The way Christopher's eyes cut to me for only the briefest of seconds made me think he had a plan, and that my father's question might just ruin it all. "I'm sure Emma will be fine. She's not a child, Sebastien."

"I know that." Dad looked at me for an answer. "Will that be okay with you if your mom and I go off for the whole weekend?"

"Yes." I took a quick glance at Christopher and saw the slightest of smiles on his lips.

"See," he said without looking at me. "She'll be fine. Hell, if she needs anything, I'll be home. She can call me."

My heart really went wild.

Was he trying to get me all alone this weekend?

I knew I was grasping at straws. There was no way that man wanted me in the way I'd been dreaming.

But what a great fantasy.

Maybe if he really didn't have any designs on me, and I would be alone all weekend, I'd buy myself a vibrator and get to know the sexual side of myself a little better. No one would be home to hear my screams of ecstasy after all.

"Well, if Emma's okay with it, then okay," Dad said, smiling. "This actually might be pretty fun. I can't recall the last time Celeste and I went on a weekend trip alone."

"Never," I blurted out. "I can't remember a single time you and Mom went anywhere alone."

Christopher blinked a few times. "Really?" he asked Dad.

"I guess she's right. Maybe it was before she was born." He shook his head. "Damn, time flies, huh?"

Finally, Christopher looked at me. "Seems it's high time they did a lot more on their own, huh, Emma?"

"Seems so," I agreed with a huge grin on my face.

When he reached out his large hand, I didn't know what he wanted. "Give me your cell, Emma."

Without hesitation, I reached into my purse, taking out my phone and placing it in his hand. "Okay."

"What's the passcode?" Christopher asked.

"A secret," I said.

Dad looked at me with an expression that told me not to make jokes. "Emma."

Christopher only smiled. "I promise that I'll forget it as soon as you tell me."

"Yeah, he's old like me; his memory isn't what it used to be," Dad had to add.

Christopher wasn't old like Dad. Not one bit. He kept his body in top shape, and he didn't look like any other man my father's age that I'd ever seen.

"Four, six, one, five," I said quietly.

As he typed that in, he asked, "What do those numbers represent?"

It felt dumb to say it out loud, but I'd never been good at lying. "Four is my favorite number. Six is the number of chin-ups I can do.

One is my best friend's favorite number. And five is the..." I didn't have a clue what to say, but knew I couldn't tell him the truth about that number. I'd recently changed the passcode to include the number of days I'd eaten with Christopher. I had to make up a lie, "... amount of pancakes I can eat in one sitting."

I wonder what he'd think if I told him the real reason behind that number.

CHAPTER 11

Christopher

I tried hard to not think about Emma during her second week at the office. I kept myself busy and didn't even go into the office until the end of the week. That was either a terrible mistake or fate. I wasn't sure which.

When I stepped off the elevator, I saw her walking down the hall, her back to me. As if by some miracle, her sweet scent still lingered in the air. I inhaled it deep into my lungs, setting myself on fire. My cock hardened immediately, and my brain went to work, trying to figure out a way to get the pretty young thing alone for the weekend.

As if by instinct, I thought of something her father could do which would take him and his wife out of town for the weekend. And then I went to work, thinking up something for Emma to do to get her out of town as well.

By Friday morning, I finally had a plan that would allow me to spend some time alone with Emma. Mrs. Kramer came into my office when I asked.

"You wanted to see me, Mr. Taylor?"

"Yes." I pulled out the packet I'd put together and slid it across my desk to her. "I want you to send Miss Hancock out to scout for activities to do and a nice place to stay in Concord this weekend for our visitors from China. They've expressed great interest in seeing the capital of New Hampshire, and they'll be here in two weeks, so we've got to get on this. After a weekend of sightseeing in Concord, we'll bring them here for our meeting on the Monday."

"Okay, sir." She picked up the packet. "I'll give her this." Turning to leave, she paused and then looked back at me. "I'll make reservations for her in Concord then."

"I already have. The Centennial is a safe, secure place for a young woman who's traveling alone." I had to fight the grin that threatened to give my plan away. "She'll be fine there."

"Yes, sir." Mrs. Kramer looked at me with a satisfied expression before adding, "It's nice to see you like this. It's been a long time since you've gotten involved in something like that. Sebastien's friendship has been good for you." And with that, she left me.

Left me to think about the only person I could count as a friend, Sebastien. Left me alone to reconsider my plan. Left me to think about everything I'd been feeling over the last two weeks and to try to regain control over emotions that were running amok for the first time in many, many years.

The twenty-six year age gap between Emma and me didn't help things one bit. There were too many factors that could mean bad news for both of us if I followed through with what I'd planned.

I'd made reservations for my own room at the hotel, which was considered one of the most romantic accommodations in the area. I'd also made dinner reservations at the Granite Restaurant inside the grand old hotel for both Friday and Saturday night.

Premeditated romance?

Could that be considered a crime?

I supposed, in Sebastien's eyes, it might well be considered a crime. At best, he'd likely think it insidious. And he might be right. I had no business wanting to be alone with his young daughter. But for the life of me, I could not stop thinking about her.

My nights were consumed with sexual fantasies about her,

making my dreams very interesting. But I had to admit that I did feel guilty sometimes after it was all said and done. Why would I go and get myself all infatuated with someone so young? And why did she have to be the daughter of the only friend I had left?

With the weekend work all set, I knew Sebastien—and now Emma—would be leaving the office at noon to get to where they needed to go. I wondered if Emma was excited by her little scouting assignment.

I almost messed up and went to see her at her office. I wanted so badly to know how she felt about the trip, but then that would be a real mess. She'd tell me all about where she was going and then, when I showed up, I most definitely would not be able to play it off like a coincidence.

For a second, doubt ran through me. *What if Mrs. Kramer tells Emma that I made all the arrangements?*

I hadn't thought it all the way through. The whole thing might backfire on me.

A little knock sounded at my door, and Mrs. Kramer stepped inside. "I wanted to tell you something that just occurred to me."

The worried look on her face made me curious. "What's just occurred to you?"

"You don't normally make the arrangements for..." she paused then shrugged, "well, anything, really. If Miss Hancock finds out that you set things up, then she might tell someone else. Then I think we'd have something here that might stir up gossip. I don't want people thinking I've been slipping at my job, and you've had to take over. So, I took credit for making the arrangements, I hope you don't mind."

I'd never felt more relieved. "Yes, you made a good judgment call there, Mrs. Kramer. I didn't even think about that. And again, you know I'm very happy with all the work you do." With a satisfied smile, she left my office.

I was glad Mrs. Kramer had taken care to cover for me, even if she did for her own reason. Convincing her to say that she'd made the reservation was not something I would've enjoyed. My assistant certainly didn't need to know the real reasons I'd set Emma up in a hotel where I would wine and dine her, dance and romance her. And if everything went right, sweep her off her feet—literally.

When my personal cell rang, it jolted me out of my inner thoughts, and I looked down to see Sebastien's name on the screen. A small amount of guilt had me hesitating to answer the call, but I really had no choice. "Hello, Sebastien. Are you and Celeste packed and ready to head out after lunch?"

"Yes, we are." He cleared his throat before going on, "Emma just came to my office and told me she's being sent to Concord to do a bit of scouting."

Is he going to be mad? "Yes, well, that's part of her job."

"Yeah, I know." He laughed. "She's over the moon about it. She was gushing about how cool it's going to be, staying in a hotel room all on her very own the next two nights. So, I guess you're off the hook."

"What hook was I on?" I asked, feeling slightly confused.

With a chuckle, he let me in on his train of thought. "You know how you told her yesterday that if she needed something that she could call you?"

"Oh, that hook." I'd totally forgotten about that whole conversation. "Well, she can still call me if she gets into a bind. Let her know that."

"She'll be fine," he said. "But I'll let her know, just in case. Thanks, buddy. You're a really great friend. I know I've told you that a lot lately, but it bears repeating."

And then the guilt really set in. "Oh, I'm nothing special." I wasn't special at all. I had an agenda, and my poor friend had no idea about the designs I had on his daughter.

But what if I was honest with him and let him in on my interest? What then?

He had to go and make things even harder for me by saying, "No, don't do that. You're very special. There aren't many like you, Christopher." He paused to let that sink in a moment before changing the subject. "So what are your weekend plans while the rest of us are out of town?"

To defile your young daughter.

I coughed as the terrible thought crossed my mind. "I think I'll stay home this weekend. My daughters are going somewhere with their mother, and the house will be quiet."

"Sounds nice. Maybe get a good book and relax on your deck and enjoy the lake and this lovely summer weather we're having. Sounds like an awesome plan you've got there." Enthusiasm filled his voice. "Enjoy, buddy. Bye now."

I put the phone down and then put my head in my hands. "I'm a monster. And now that Sebastien knows that I know where Emma will be for the weekend, my whole plan is ruined." I hadn't counted on Emma telling her father everything. Seemed I hadn't thought things through at all.

In my defense, I hadn't had a romantic tryst in forever and then some. To call myself rusty was a vast understatement. It seemed I was clueless.

The Governor's Suite I'd booked would go empty. The dinner reservations would have to be cancelled. And I would have the saddest weekend I'd had in a while.

I was no stranger to lonely weekends, but I knew this one would be even worse than the sad ones I'd lived through after I found out Lisa had cheated on me with every man I knew.

At least those weekends had had some relief to them. They signified the end to my loveless marriage. And the best part about it was that she'd done wrong, and that meant I wouldn't have to hand Lisa everything I'd worked so hard for.

This weekend the only plans I could imagine would involve sitting around alone, wondering what Emma was doing. Wondering if she was having fun and looking beautiful as she toured the town.

I could imagine her golden-brown hair swept up in a high ponytail, blowing in the warm summer breeze as she strolled the sidewalks of downtown Concord. Her pink lips would pull into a smile every time she caught her reflection in a window pane. And I wanted to be there, just on the other side of her, seeing it all with her. Holding her soft hand, our fingers entwined, kissing her hand once in a while as we walked and talked.

Why can't I be twenty again?

How come I've got to be old enough to be her father?

Sitting in my chair, I spun around like a restless little kid and wished that things could be different—that they could be just the way I wanted them. That Emma and I could be together and no one would judge—or worse, make things hell for us.

But I knew Hell was the only thing in store for us if we ever did get to the place I desperately wished for. We'd get it from both sides. Her parents, my daughters, and most likely the staff at my company, too.

The staff I could handle. The other parties I wasn't so sure.

And there I was again, getting ahead of myself. I didn't know if Emma even felt the same interest in me that I felt for her. I knew enough from my own kids to know that their generation thought thirty was old.

Forty-six would seem ancient to a woman as young as Emma.

Feeling a heaviness in my chest, I let doubt, fear, and insecurity creep in without even trying to combat any of it.

I'd be alone for the rest of my life. But, just a few weeks ago, I had rejoiced in that. But now that I'd glimpsed something so special with Emma, I knew that that's what I wanted.

And I knew I wouldn't ever find any other woman who would do to me what Emma had done. But none of that mattered. What mattered was Emma. She didn't need the war that a relationship with me would cause. She didn't need a rift between her and the parents who adored her. And she sure as hell didn't need the wrath of my daughters.

My plans were officially dead. I couldn't go through with it. I couldn't put such an innocent girl into such a tricky situation. I didn't know if she'd agree with me or not, but I knew it was the right thing to do.

I had to put her back into the far recesses of my mind, shut her in, and never open that door again.

CHAPTER 12

Emma

After running home at lunchtime to pack, I kissed Mom and Dad goodbye before they got into Dad's company car; I got into mine, and we all headed off to our work weekends. To some, a weekend away for work may have sounded boring, but to us it sounded like fun.

I'd never gone on a trip alone before. Mom was a little worried about me, but I told her that I had my cell and that meant I had GPS, and they would know my whereabouts at all times. It eased her mind some. Dad said he'd already thought of that, and that's why he'd felt comfortable with me making the trip.

I'd secretly rolled my eyes at that. While I never wanted to worry my parents unnecessarily, I was a working professional now; I would take work trips whether Dad felt comfortable about them or not.

When Mrs. Kramer came into my office with the packet she'd put together for my excursion, my bubble burst just a bit. I'd honestly thought Christopher might've had an agenda, sending my father and mother away. But I'd been wrong, it seemed. He had no plans for me at all—other than work plans, it seemed.

The brief interaction I'd had with him the day before had left me with enough of a glimpse of his skin and his body that my dreams were the sweetest ever: visions filled with the two of us lying on a beach, running our hands over each other's bodies, kissing tenderly.

Sure, I didn't know what any of that really felt like, since I'd never done any of it before, but it didn't seem to matter in my little dream-world. Nothing mattered in my dream-world.

If by some miracle Christopher Taylor did want me the way I wanted him, there would be so many obstacles in our way. Somehow, I didn't care. If it meant I got to be with Christopher, I could deal with anything. Not that I thought I would ever get that chance, but it was a pleasant fantasy, and it kept me going.

The thirty-minute drive to the Centennial Hotel passed in a flash. Walking up to the entrance, I admired the red brick structure that I'd read had been opened in 1876 as a home for elderly residents who didn't have enough money to live on their own. Later it was transformed into a luxury hotel. And now I was getting to stay in it, thanks to my fabulous job.

Entering the lobby, I felt as if I'd stepped back in time, the building's long history seeming to hang heavy in the air.

"Good afternoon, miss," the receptionist greeted me with a smile. "How are you doing today?"

"Great, actually. I'm Emma Hancock. My company made a reservation for me." I put my suitcase down only for a bellhop to appear out of nowhere to pick it up for me.

"I'll escort you to your room, miss," he told me.

I could handle my one suitcase on my own, but I let the young man do his job while the receptionist looked up the reservation.

"Oh, yes. You're in one of our turret suites on the third floor. Jason will show you to it." She handed me a keycard. "It's the King Turret, Jason. Thank you for staying with us, Miss Hancock. If you'd like to dine in our restaurant, you can make reservations using the phone in your suite. Or you can order in, and we'll have it brought to you."

"Thank you. I'll see what I feel like doing once I get settled in." Following Jason to the stairs, I took in a deep breath. The air felt electric, like something special was about to happen.

Even though my plans were pretty mundane—I'd be touring the town and finding things our Chinese guests would hopefully find exciting and pleasing—I felt a charge that couldn't be explained.

When we got up to the room, my jaw dropped as I looked around. "This is so beautiful."

Jason put my suitcase just inside the door. "Glad you like it. If there's anything you need, please call the front desk and we'll bring it right up to you. We've got every toiletry you can imagine if you've forgotten anything."

I reached into my purse, pulling out a five dollar bill. "Thank you so much, Jason. You've been very helpful. If I need anything, I will call."

With a smile and a wave, he closed the door, leaving me alone. The first thing I did was look at the vast king-size bed. I kicked off my shoes and ran to flop down on it. "Oh, how soft!"

Running my hands over the bedspread, I nuzzled a thick, plush pillow and thought I might just take a little nap. A few minutes would be all I'd need.

Two hours later, I woke with a start. My cell was ringing, my mother's name flashing on the screen. "Hi, Mom. I made it all right," I croaked.

"Were you sleeping, Emma?" she asked, sounding surprised.

"The first thing I did was fall on the bed—this is the comfiest bed I've ever laid down on, and this is the most magnificent room I've ever been in. It seems I did fall asleep. I guess I needed to catch up a bit." I rubbed my eyes as I sat up. "What time is it?"

"Four," she said. "Have you made reservations for dinner yet? Your father said that if you're going to eat in the room, which is what he'd prefer, then you should make reservations at the hotel restaurant. He doesn't want you out exploring an unfamiliar city after dark."

Man, he really knows how to make me feel like a baby!

"I don't want to go eat alone in some fancy restaurant, Mom. I'll get room-service." Wondering how long it would be until it got dark, I looked out the window to see where the sun was. "I've got things I need to do before it gets dark. I might just pick up something from a drive-thru and bring it back here to eat."

Dad called out in the background, "You don't need to eat crap, Emma. Get something healthy. And put it all on the company card. You don't have to spend your own money on things like this."

"I know, Dad. Mrs. Kramer told me that already. She's told me everything I need to know." I rolled my eyes even though no one could see me. Sometimes my parents could exasperate me. "I can handle this—and myself. How about we give each other some space this weekend? I'll check in each night by text, and then we'll see each other at home on Sunday evening."

"Are you sure about that, sweetie?" Mom asked. "You've never been alone that long."

"Yeah, I know. I'm perfectly safe here. No reason for anyone to worry about me, okay?" I reassured them as I went to the bathroom. "I'm going to freshen up then head out. I'll text you tomorrow night."

"No," came Dad's answer to that. "Tonight, too. Around nine or so. Not any later than ten. Got it?"

"Sure." I couldn't expect miracles. "Bye." I ended the call then placed the phone on the vanity as I looked at my reflection. "Hmm, yup. You look like an adult. Why don't they see you like one?"

After running the straightener through my hair, I washed my face then applied a little mascara, some pink lip gloss, and added a little blush to top it all off. I changed into a pink sundress and some tan flats, then left the room to go take a tour of the town.

Walking down the stairs, I felt that charge in the air again. The hotel must've seen some pretty amazing people in its time. At least that's what I chalked the energy up to.

Just before I entered the lobby, I heard a deep voice that seemed familiar. And as I rounded the corner, I saw why. "Christopher," I whispered.

His head turned as if he'd heard me. Then a smile pulled his chiseled lips up at each corner. "Emma, how's it going?"

"Um. I...um," I stammered, having no idea how it was going.

The bellhop was the same guy who'd helped me. He stood on the other side of Christopher, who turned to tell him, "Take my things up, please. I'll be up later." Then Christopher came toward me. "So, how do you like Concord so far, Emma?"

"I took a nap," I blurted out like some kind of idiot.

"A nap?" He came to stand right in front of me. His expensive cologne tickled my nostrils. "This schedule is new to you. I'm sure you needed to catch up on your sleep."

"What are you doing here?" I asked, my body tingling at the thought that we'd be spending the night under the same roof.

"Just a little getaway. My daughters went on some excursion with their mother, and I was home alone." He shifted his weight then looked past me. "I wanted a change of scenery."

"Wow." My parents had told me that the scenery from his mansion was to die for. "I guess you don't like to be alone much, do you?"

His eyes came back to mine. "It's never bothered me. It wasn't that I didn't want to be alone, I just wanted to do something a little different, that's all."

Then I realized that he probably wanted to be alone to enjoy his getaway, and I was getting in his way. "Well, I'll get out of your way then and leave you to it." I turned to walk away, but his hand on my shoulder stopped me.

"That's okay. I actually came here so you wouldn't feel so alone in this place. I've made dinner reservations at Granite, here in the hotel." He ran his hand from my shoulder down my arm before pulling away, leaving a trail of fire in its wake. "I'd like for you to join me, if you can. The reservation is at eight."

"You want me to join you?" I asked with surprise, shaking my head in disbelief.

"Yes, please." He smiled at me again, and it made my heart skip a beat. "Or would you hate to be seen in the company of an old man like me?"

"Old man?" He was anything but that in my eyes. "I wouldn't hate to be seen in your company at all. And I don't think you're an old man, either. I thought it might be embarrassing for you to be seen with me."

His smile turned into a frown. "And why's that, Emma?"

Shrugging, I didn't know quite how to put it. "Just 'cause I'm a nobody kid, I guess."

With a sigh, he looked me right in the eyes. "You're not a kid, and you're not a nobody." He took me by the chin, his thumb rubbing my skin the slightest bit. "And I would be the envy of all the men in the restaurant if you would join me for dinner."

"You would?" I couldn't believe he'd said such a thing.

"I would," he said, He moved his hand away from my face, and I felt its loss in every part of my body.

The thought of spending the evening with this man sent a bolt of sensation through me. My panties felt wet, my entire body vibrated, and something was happening in my nether regions that had never happened before.

"Is it a formal dress code?" I asked. I hadn't brought anything formal.

"What you have on now is perfect, Emma." He chuckled quietly, the sound deep and sexy. "Are you trying to make excuses to not join me?"

"No." I wasn't doing that at all. I just couldn't rationalize why he'd want to eat dinner with me. "My father might not approve, Mr. Taylor."

"What's this Mr. Taylor stuff?" He took my chin in between his fingers again. "I thought we'd already discussed that. When we're not at work, you're Emma and I'm Christopher. And as far as your father's approval goes, I don't see him here, and you're not a baby. So, will you join me for dinner or leave me to dine alone this evening?"

I didn't know what to say, so I just nodded, to which he frowned. I could see that my way of answering wasn't enough for him, so I said, "Okay, I'll join you for dinner."

And that was that—my first date. If that's what it really was.

A girl could dream.

CHAPTER 13

Christopher

I didn't recall ever being so—for lack of a better word—giddy. This wasn't exactly a feeling I was used to.

Eight o'clock came around, and I left my room to meet Emma in the lobby as we'd planned. My heart raced with each step I took.

I'm really doing this!

Or was I?

This dinner could be orchestrated any way I wanted it. I could set the tone of a friendly meal with my friend's daughter. Or I could make it a boss/employee kind of thing. But what I really wanted to do was put the ball in her court and see where things might lead.

Emma stood near the entrance to the restaurant, her head bowed as she looked at the screen of the cell phone in her hand. I cleared my throat to attract her attention. Looking up, she turned her head toward me and a smile transformed her pretty face.

"Hi." She waved with one hand and slipped her phone into her purse with the other.

"Hi," I said as I came to stand next to her.

A flowery scent drifted around her as she moved toward the

restaurant. "The smells coming out of this place are making my tummy growl."

The smell she gave off made my loins stir. I put my hand on the small of her back. "I'm glad you like it so far, Emma." Even that brief contact was enough to make my palm tingle and my cock stir. Thankfully, the jacket of my suit covered that well.

The host greeted us, "Your reservation is for?"

"Taylor," I said, then trailed my hand up Emma's back to rest it on her shoulder. "For two."

"Perfect," the man said as he gathered some menus. "Right this way," he led us to a small table near a window with a pleasant view. The only view I was interested in was that of my companion for the evening.

"May I get you something from the bar while you look over the menu?" the host asked as Emma and I took our seats next to each other.

With a quick glance at the cocktail menu, I made the order for us both, "We'll have a couple of your Forbidden Sours, thank you."

The host left us to put in our order with the bartender, and Emma leaned toward me, a small frown on her adorable face. "Christopher, you might have forgotten this," she said in a whisper, "but I'm only twenty. Not old enough to drink yet."

"I won't tell if you won't," I teased her.

She sat back, a blush staining her cheeks. "I've had a little bit of wine with my mom and dad. I guess this will be okay too. But promise me you won't tell my father, please. He'd definitely have something to say about it."

There were so many things I would never tell her father, so that promise would be easy to keep. "Sure thing, Emma. This will be our little secret."

She looked over the menu with wide eyes. "Oh, these prices are out of this world. I can't even look at the dishes because my eyes keep getting stuck on how much they cost."

"Order whatever you want, Emma. This is on the company, remember?" I asked as I grinned at her.

"But, I just can't make myself do it," she said then put the menu down. "Would you mind ordering for me?"

My cock grew a little more at her request. There was nothing sexier than the thought of her putting herself in my hands, trusting me. "Alright, Emma. Do you like beef, chicken, or seafood?"

"Seafood," came her quick reply. "In order of preference, I like seafood, any kind at all, then chicken, and then beef. And if you're going for a steak, then it has to be fully cooked, no pink."

"I see." I put the menu down, as I already knew what I wanted. "I'll have to make you a steak at my place sometime. Rare is the only way to truly enjoy steaks. And I make a mean one on my outdoor grill. I'll bet if you had a properly cooked steak, you'd like it."

"I don't know," she said as she wrinkled her nose and made a funny face. "Bloody meat is kind of...well, gross."

"You'll see. Maybe Sunday you can come over, and I'll make dinner for you before your parents get back." I knew setting up another time for us to be alone might be pushing it, but I had to try.

She eyed me warily, making me a little nervous. "Christopher, I'm still not ready to meet your daughters if that's what you're up to."

Relief washed over me. "Oh, I'm not trying to do that, Emma. Not at all. They won't be home until late Sunday evening, or maybe even Monday sometime. It would just be you and I." Then I got nervous that would scare her off.

She seemed to consider her answer as she looked up at the chandelier hovering over our table. "Well then, that sounds like fun." Her eyes came to rest on mine. "But don't be upset if I don't like the steak, okay?"

I had another date with her; nothing would make me upset. "I promise not to get upset with you, Emma."

Our waiter came to us with our drinks. "Good evening, Mr. Taylor. I'm Raphael, and I'll be your server this evening." He placed Emma's drink in front her as he smiled at her. "And what may I call you this evening, miss?"

"Emma," she said with a shy smile.

"Well, Emma, it's a pleasure to serve you this evening." He bowed, and I could see from the grin on his face that he liked the looks of my dinner companion. And he must've thought I was her father or something and not any kind of competition, because he slid my drink to me without so much as glancing my way. I had to admit, that bothered me a hell of a lot.

"We'd like to start things off with the artisanal cheese plate, followed by the New England clam chowder, then for the main course we'll both have the seared scallops with smoked ham." My words came out sharper than I meant.

He finally pulled his dark eyes off Emma to look at me. "I'll put that order in right away." He took the menus, leaving behind the dessert menu. "And I'll leave that for you, sir."

"Thank you." I slid the menu to Emma. "I think you can decide on a desert."

As the boy left us, I wondered if Emma thought he was as cute as he thought she was. But I didn't say a word as she looked over the menu.

"These all looks so delicious." She put the menu down. "But I hardly ever eat sweets. My parents don't keep much sugar in the house, and it's probably for the best." She ran her fingertips over her cheek. "As you can see, I have trouble with my weight."

"Are you kidding?" I had to ask. Then it just popped out, "You're perfect. Round in all the right places." Then I clamped my mouth shut tightly.

That's not something you're supposed to say on a first date, you idiot!

The way her eyes went soft made my entire body stiffen. "Do you really think that? Or are you just being nice, Christopher?"

I felt like my foot was caught in a bear trap, and I had no idea how to get it out. I probably shouldn't have said anything about how great I thought she looked. But then again, the girl needed to know that she was a knockout. "I really think that."

She made a crooked smile. "I've never thought of myself as round in all the right places. I've thought of myself as plump. And to be honest, no one has ever told me otherwise."

"Well, that's a damn shame, Emma." I felt myself loosening up as

I remembered the young lady sitting across the small table from me was still extremely innocent. She had been kept under her father's wing for far too long, and she needed to know how beautiful she really was. "I happen to think that you're remarkably beautiful."

Her face went beet red, and she ducked her head. "Oh, stop it!"

The way she'd reacted did something to me. Testosterone flooded through me as I admired her shy blush. That wasn't the kind of reaction a woman has when being told she was beautiful if she wasn't attracted to the man. No, her reaction told me that she liked what I'd said. And that meant she might feel the attraction between us, too.

But I didn't want to push things with her. I eased off on the charm. "Okay, I'll stop, Emma. I can see you're not used to being complimented. I don't want to embarrass you—but for the record, you deserve to be showered with compliments."

The waiter came back with the cheese plate, and he noticed that Emma hadn't touched her drink. Nor had I for that matter, but he didn't seem to see my full glass. "Would you like me to get you something else from the bar, Emma?"

She looked up at him, shaking her head, "No, thank you."

He pointed at her glass. "It's just that you haven't touched your cocktail. The Forbidden Sour isn't usually favored by our younger guests, and it's not a problem to get you something more your style."

My skin began to feel prickly as the guy leaned in too close to her. "Hey there, buddy." The waiter looked at me for once. "If she wants something else, I'll let you know. Back up a bit. She's here with me, not you."

His face fell a bit. "My apologies, sir. I didn't realize, you were here...together?"

Emma took the lead as she answered, "Yes, we are. This drink is fine with me. He wanted me to try it, and I want to try it. Besides, I'm a bit of an old soul. I like the tried and true things."

My cock jerked so hard I thought it might rip my slacks.

Does this mean she's into me?

"Sorry," he said, then walked away with his tail between his legs.

"So am I," I said, looking back to Emma. "I've overstepped my bounds, Emma. I shouldn't have said anything." I had my fingers crossed under the table, hoping that she'd put my fears at ease.

She cocked her head to one side, looking puzzled. "Why?"

Why? "Because you might have been interested in that kid."

Leaning forward to rest her face on her hand as she propped her elbow on the table, I swore I saw her eyes sparkle with flirtation.

"I'm not usually interested in *kids*, Christopher. I've never met one single young man who made my heart thump hard in my chest, or who ignited a fire in my veins." She picked up a piece of cheese then put it into her mouth.

I sat back, wondering how to respond to that. Finally, I asked, "Have you ever met anyone at all who made you feel those things, Emma?"

Her long, dark lashes closed as she averted her eyes, "I have now."

Holy shit!

CHAPTER 14

Emma

Not an ounce of liquid courage in me and I'd said more to Christopher than I'd ever planned to. With the moment of truth at hand, I held my breath, waiting to hear how he'd respond to my bold statement.

I felt his fingertips graze over the top of my hand, which rested near the cocktail that had sparked this conversation in the first place. "Am I the one who's sparked those things, Emma?"

Like a volcanic eruption, heat filled me. My next words exploded out of my mouth on a raspy exhalation. "I've never wanted anyone as much as I want you."

He closed his hand over mine, and I could feel the intense heat coming off him. "I've got to admit the same thing to you, Emma."

Slowly, I opened my eyes and raised my head to look at him. "Is that true?" It was too hard to believe that he might share my desire. "I'm young. Inexperienced. It's a little…taboo, isn't it?"

"I know you're young and innocent." Christopher bit his lower lip. "And I haven't stopped thinking about you since I first laid my eyes on you." He moved his hand around mine until our fingers were entwined. "Can I ask how long you've felt this way about me?"

"The same," I admitted. "Since I first saw you. But I honestly never imagined you'd be attracted to me as well."

"I've never been so attracted to anyone, Emma." He looked me right in the eyes and I thought I saw his sincerity, but I still couldn't make myself believe his words.

"Don't," I whispered. "Don't tell me anything that's not true. You've been married, Christopher; you must've felt this kind of attraction before." I didn't want to think about his ex-wife, but I didn't want him to lie to me either.

With a huff, he tugged my hand, pulling it off the small table and placing it on his upper thigh, hidden by the tablecloth. I could feel his thick cock underneath the fabric of his slacks. I held my breath as heat flushed through me.

"You do that to me, Emma. Only you. So many years have passed, and no one has stirred me the way you do. I've never felt like this for anyone, and I do mean *anyone*. Not even her. I know you must know about my ex."

With a nod, I tried to take sips of air as our eyes stayed locked. Feeling the length of his cock beneath my fingers, I was frozen, but I managed to say, "I do. She sounds like a real bitch. I don't normally call anyone names, but she deserves it."

"Yes, she does." He moved my hand up further until I felt the entire hot length of his erection. His head dipped close to mine, his breath in my ear making me shiver. "So, can you believe me when I say no one has ever done this to me before?"

"I'm beginning to believe you, Christopher." I nearly cried in disappointment as he moved our clasped hands back to the tabletop. I looked at my hand, the one that touched him in a way I'd never touched any man. "What does this mean?"

"Whatever you want it to mean," he replied with a sexy grin. "You're in control, Emma. I don't want to rush you into anything. I'm assuming, your father being the way he is, that you haven't dated, much less had sex."

"Please," I begged as I arched my back to grind my pelvis against his cock.

Soft bites traveled up my neck and then his hot breath tickled my ear again. "We're going to go slow, baby. You've got so much to experience. I'm not going to rush that for you."

Oh, but I wanted to rush. "Please," I begged him. "Just take me."

A low chuckle made his chest rumble against mine. "I will. But first, I'll make you feel things you've never felt before."

I wanted to cry with frustration at the thought of having to wait, but then he moved with me, leading me to the bed, laying me down gently across it. Struggling to catch my breath, I looked at him, watching him as he looked me over.

His hands moved under my dress and he lifted it up, taking it off me in one smooth motion. Only a pink bra and matching panties covered my body, my flats having been abandoned at some point.

His chest rose and fell as his breaths came hard and heavy. He pulled off his jacket, letting it fall to the floor He ripped the buttons off his shirt as he tore it off. His slacks were tented by his huge erection, and I couldn't wait to see what they held. He undid his pants, then pushed them to the floor.

My heart beat so hard I could hear it. "I want to see."

He smiled, then dropped his boxer briefs, letting me see his gorgeous cock for the first time. "There you go, baby."

My mouth watered at the sight. "Oh, God!"

"I'm going to sink this cock so far into your sweet cunt you won't know where you end and I begin." He reached down, taking either side of my panties and ripping them right off me. With one hand, he did the same to my bra.

Speechless, I just looked up at him. His handsome, usually friendly face had morphed into that of a sex-driven beast—a sexy as hell beast, but still a beast. He grabbed my ankles next, tugging them until my knees bent. Then he climbed onto the bed, moving between my legs.

Unsure of what he was about to do, I closed my eyes. "Just do it,

Christopher. I've waited so long..." I gasped as I felt his hot mouth on my sex. "God!"

His hands gripped my ass as he lifted me up off the bed to bring me closer to his mouth, licking, sucking, and even biting me into a frenzied state. I couldn't help myself as I screamed with desire; I was overwhelmed with feelings that I couldn't put a name to.

I'd never been so wet. I'd never felt so much at once. My mind didn't know how to handle it all. When his tongue pushed into me, I felt something odd happening inside of me.

Almost like a wave, a feeling started deep in my belly. It moved, flowing through me, tingling and pulsing up to my head and down to my toes that curled as I lost all control. I grabbed Christopher's shoulders as I had my first orgasm, shouting his name as I burst apart. "Yes! God, yes! Christopher!"

Slowly, he stopped what he'd been doing, kissing me lightly all over my pulsing sex before pulling his head up to look at me. "Did you like that, baby?"

Nodding, panting, I fell back on the pillows, realizing for the first time that I'd been propped up on my elbows, watching him as he ate me out. "Very much." Exhaustion took over, and I lay back, closing my eyes. "I'm going to need a break."

"Yeah, I thought as much." He moved to lay next to me, propping his head on his hand as he looked down at me, his fingertips trailing gently over my breast. His lips pressed against my cheek as he murmured against my skin, "You know we've got to keep this a secret, right?"

I opened my eyes, looking at him. "I do know that. My parents will want to kill you."

"And my daughters will want to do the same to you." He kissed my lips so tenderly it made a tear slip from my eye. This was like nothing I'd ever experienced before. "But we can have this. No one needs to know."

Moving my hand up his muscular arm to rest on his bicep, I felt a pain in my heart. "How long can we have this for, Christopher?"

"For as long as we both want it." He kissed me again. "If you're asking me how long I'll want it, I know I'll want it for a very long time."

Chewing my lip, I wondered how long we could have anything if we had to keep it a secret. And then doubt, as well as a good amount of despair, filled me. "I think I should go to my room now. This is…a lot. I don't know if I can do this."

He tried to stop me. "Wait!"

Jumping up, I grabbed my dress off the floor and flung it on, not bothering with my bra or panties. I scooped up my purse and ran out of his room, which was only a few doors down from mine, thankfully.

I just can't do this!

CHAPTER 15

Christopher

As Emma left my room, I sat there shocked and speechless. I didn't know what to do. All I knew was that I wanted her more than ever, and I knew she had to want me too.

I knew it was the secrecy of it all that had stopped her from letting anything more happen between us. I didn't know how to get around that, though. No matter what scenario I imagined to tell her parents about my feelings for Emma, nothing seemed like it would work.

How was someone supposed to approach their friend with that kind of information? *'Oh, hey, Sebastien, I really like your daughter, so she and I are going to start hitting it hard and heavy. Okay, ol' buddy?"*

I could just imagine how that would end—with me on the floor after a well-deserved punch to the face.

Needless to say, the rest of the weekend passed with no contact between us. After trying to find Emma the next day with no luck—she must've been avoiding me—I decided to head home. And there was no second date at my lake house either.

Two weeks after our explosive night together, Emma and I were at a standstill. Even though Emma and I would be polite to one another at the office, I could tell not one thing had changed for either of us. I could read it in her body language and her eyes when she looked at me—she still wanted me as much as I wanted her.

Staring out the window one afternoon, I turned to look at the door as someone knocked. "Come in."

In came Sebastien, and he looked irritated. Alarm bells went off immediately. *Did she tell him about Concord?*

"I need to talk to you, Christopher." He slammed his fist into his palm. "There's a son-of-a-bitch nosing around my little girl, and I want that to stop. Please tell me you can do something about it. It's inappropriate in the workplace."

I didn't want anyone nosing around his daughter either. "I can. Who is it that's bothering Emma?"

"Randy from accounting." He took a seat, then tapped his foot relentlessly, his protective instincts apparently getting the better of him. "And he's gone so far as to follow her back to her office to ask her out on a lunch date, the little weasel."

I took my seat behind my desk. "I see." Jealousy started to build up in me, but I knew I had to try to be reasonable. "Did she tell you that he was bothering her? Or is it just you who has a problem with it, Sebastien?"

He shook his head. "No, she told me about it and asked me how she could make him stop. I told her not to worry, that I would handle it. She pleaded with me not to embarrass her, and said I should come to you for help."

"Oh, she did?" I knew then for certain that she wanted me to stop it, and that made me very happy. "Well, I'll have someone from HR tell the kid that his behavior is inappropriate, and if he pursues it further, it will be considered sexual harassment. If he values his job, which let's hope he does, that should be deterrent enough."

Sebastien calmed down right away. "Emma was right. It was best to come to you with this problem."

"Yes, she was." I couldn't help but feel a little hope that like this meant she might want to see me again.

"She admires you, you know," he went on to say. "She talks about you a lot."

My interest piqued, I asked, "She does?"

"Yeah," he said as he got up to leave. "She feels very bad about how your ex did you. We saw Lisa walking down the sidewalk last weekend, by the way. I pointed her out and Emma mumbled something about running her over."

So, she's jealous, too.

"That's nice of her," I mumbled.

Sebastien laughed. "Nice? I wouldn't say that. I told her that wasn't a nice thing to say, much less think."

With a shrug, I admitted, "I've thought about the same thing myself once or twice."

"Yeah, but that's you." He headed toward the door. "Emma doesn't have any reason to want that woman dead." Opening the door, he reminded me with a tight smile, "Please get on with Operation Reduce Randy's Presence in My Daughter's Life. The sooner, the better, in my opinion."

Mine too. "I'm making the call to HR now."

After getting that taken care of, I decided to head home. On Thursdays, Emma usually picked up my dry cleaning and took it to my place. So, it being Thursday, I knew I'd run into her at home, and then we could have a little discussion.

We had to come to some kind of agreement or I would go crazy. That one taste of her had only served to make me want her more. And I knew she wanted it too.

A little while later, I sat in the foyer waiting for Emma to arrive. Whenever she came over, she placed my clean laundry in the closet in that room, so I knew I'd catch her.

The door opened and in came Emma. She was holding the plastic covered suits so high in the air that she didn't see me until she'd placed everything in the closet. When she turned, she found me standing in front of the door I'd closed. "Hello, Emma."

Her jaw dropped, and she shook her head. "No, Christopher."

"I'm not going to touch you." I crossed my arms over my chest. It wasn't that I didn't want to touch her. I wanted to pull her into my arms more than anything, but I didn't want her to feel threatened at all. "I just want to talk."

"About what?" She looked over her shoulder as if looking for an escape route.

I knew she'd never been in my home, other than that front room. "I'm not going to hurt you, Emma. There's no need to run from me."

Looking back at me, she nodded. "I know you won't. It's just that —well, to be honest, I don't trust myself around you when we're alone."

I liked hearing that. "Because you want me."

She nodded again. "Yes. But I don't like the idea of hiding things."

"Me neither." I held out my hand but didn't take a step toward her. "Can you come with me so we can just sit and talk a little?"

With a heavy sigh, she agreed. "Okay."

When I took her hand, I felt it all over again—the flush of electricity that moved through me. "I've missed you."

"I've seen you nearly every day," she said as a smile moved over her pretty face.

Pulling her hand to my mouth, I kissed it. "You know what I mean, baby."

"I've missed you too," she whispered, as if someone could overhear her, other than me.

I took a seat on a chair in the living room off the foyer and pulled her to sit on my lap. Stroking her soft hair, I breathed in her scent. "We can figure something out. I know we can."

She placed her hands on my cheeks as she looked at me, desperation filling her face. "My parents will never approve."

"I know." I took one of her hands then pulled it to my lips, kissing it softly again, loving the way goosebumps pimpled her flesh. I ran my other hand over her arm to feel them. "Keeping things to ourselves might seem like the wrong thing to do, but it's the easiest right now. That way I won't have to fight with your parents, and you won't have to fight with my daughters. They can be just as bad as their mother when they want to be."

Her green eyes danced as she looked at me. "So how would we do it then?"

The fact that she even asked the question had me thinking she didn't have much of an argument to make. I'd been toying with an idea, and I let her in on it. "We could get a little place. No one would need to know about it. On weekends, you could make some excuse, like you're going to see a friend back in Rhode Island or something. I can make up excuses for things I'm going off to do too. No one has to know that we're meeting at our love nest."

"A love nest?" she asked with shining eyes. "That sounds kind of romantic."

"I think it sounds very romantic." I traced my fingers down her long neck then over her soft lips. "I want you, Emma. I want as much of you as I can have. If that means only on weekends, then I'll take it."

"It'd be like we're together for real," she said then ran her hands through my hair. "I'd like that."

Kissing her softly, I resisted the temptation to let it go further, even though I really wanted to carry her up to my bedroom. When our mouths parted, I could barely breathe. "I'll get something as soon as I possibly can. If I get something by this weekend, will you come?"

She looked surprised. "Do you really think you can get something so soon? It's already Thursday, you know?"

"Money speeds things up, baby." I kissed her again because I couldn't help it. Her body melted into mine, and her heart pounded against my chest.

I ran my hand up her body, cupping her tit as I slipped the other between her legs, relishing the heat that came off her aroused pussy. I would get to have it very soon. A virgin. This woman who'd never been touched by any other man would belong to me. But no one could ever know.

Even as my arousal grew, my brain asked me what I was doing. A relationship between Emma and I would never be accepted by either of our families. Not ever.

Would spending the weekends together as lovers be enough? Was it a smart thing to do, or was it just courting disaster? The last thing I wanted was for us to end up hurting each other. Or would it all work out somehow?

Squirming on my lap, Emma pulled her skirt up and took my hand, moving it into her damp panties. My fingers ran through her hot folds as our kiss took a passionate turn.

Shy little Emma seemed to be disappearing as sexy, needy Emma came out to play. My cock went hard for her, but I wasn't about to take the girl's virginity like this. I wanted it to be special for her. She was giving up so much for me as it was. I didn't want that moment to be any less special for her than it was for any other girl.

But I'd give her another orgasm to keep her yearning for me. Shoving one finger into her tight pussy, I pumped it in and out of her as I palmed the rest of her sex. Writhing with need, she rode my finger, moaning delightfully as she did.

I'd never seen anything so sexy.

I felt her body clenching around my finger as she climaxed, and she pulled her mouth from mine then buried her face in my shoulder, moaning, "Christopher! Yes!"

Her juices leaked out onto my pants as they ran down my hand. I couldn't stop myself from sucking the juices off my finger—I had to taste her again. Then I ran that finger up inside of her again before putting it into her mouth.

She sucked it as she moaned. Her tongue ran around it as I pumped it between her lips a little, mimicking how I'd like her to suck my cock. Whispering, I told her, "Next time I want you to take my cock into your sweet mouth and suck me off just like that."

I pulled my finger out of her mouth as she pulled her face up to look at me. "Why wait until next time?"

Holy fuck! What am I going to do with this woman?

CHAPTER 16

Emma

Christopher quickly found a place we could rent, so I had to come up with an excuse to leave for the weekend. With a phone call to Valerie, I let her in a little on what I was up to. "Hi, I need you to lie for me if my parents call you for any reason."

"Sure," came her quick reply. "But you've gotta tell me why?"

No one could know about Christopher and me, so I worded it delicately. "I met a guy."

"Oh, hell!" she shouted. "And you need me to be your cover. I'm in!"

My prayers had been answered. "I was hoping you'd say that. I can't tell you much about him, just that he's sexy, fun, and great in every way that counts."

"Have you guys done it?" she asked.

"Not all the way." I closed my eyes as I remembered the previous day's activities. "But we've done a lot."

"You've gotta give me details, girl," she demanded.

"Well, we've kissed," I teased her.

"Come on, Emma!"

"Okay, okay," I said then flopped on my bed to spill the details. Mom and Dad had gone out to dinner, and I knew no one would overhear me. "He gave me oral sex, and I had my first 'O' and then a couple weeks later, he fingered me until I came again. Then I sucked his dick, and he came in my mouth, and I swallowed it all without even gagging a little bit."

"No way!" she shrieked.

"But this weekend we're finally going to have sex." I rolled over onto my stomach as I thought about how he'd do it. "He's found a little place we can spend our weekends at. Our love nest as we call it. And we're planning on spending all our weekends there. It's just easier to keep my parents out of this. And that's why I need you."

"I always knew they would get in your way of becoming a woman, Emma. So, I'm proud to lie to them for you if need be," I felt a rush of relief at her words.

"Good. If you get a call from them, just say that I've been with you every weekend." I thought about it for a second, wondering just how far they'd go if they ever got suspicious. "Wait, what if they call your parents?"

"Oh, that's not a problem," she assured me. "See, Mom caught Dad flirting with some old girlfriends on Facebook, and they got in some big argument. Anyway, long story short, they both got new phone numbers, so your parents won't be able to reach them."

"Great!" I thought about what I'd said and tried again. "Not great about your Dad and the old girlfriends, but about my parents not having their numbers. I'm sorry about that other stuff, and if you need to talk about it you know I'm here…"

"Oh it's fine, they love making each other jealous every once in a while." She paused for a moment as if she was thinking hard about something. "Please be careful though, Emma," she cautioned. "I mean, don't let this guy do anything to you that you don't want. And if he treats you badly, then definitely tell your dad about him."

"I don't think he'll treat me badly or do anything to me that I don't want." Mostly because there wasn't a single thing I could think of that I didn't want Christopher to do to me. "But I will tell Dad if I think I need to."

"Good. I don't much like the secrecy of all this, but I know your dad." It felt good to have someone who understood me the way Val did.

"Okay then, I'm going to text them and tell them I'm heading to see you right now. I'm telling them I'll be back late on Sunday night." I thought about it a second and then added, "Where are you going to be this weekend so that I can tell them the truth about that, at least?"

"I'm staying on campus this weekend. There's a bunch of freshmen who'll be coming to school here in the fall, and I'm giving them the whole tour of the campus." She sighed, then added, "I guess I won't see much of you anymore, now that you've gotten yourself a secret boyfriend."

"I've promised him I'll spend every weekend with him, but I'm sure I can make an exception to see you every now and then." The thought that I might become distant with my best friend made me a little sad. But then I thought about seeing Christopher and that all went away. "Okay, I've gotta get the heck out of here before they come home. I've never lied to their faces before, so I want to be gone before that happens."

"Okay, have fun."

Ending the call, I grabbed the bag I'd already packed and headed out to my car. Just before I pulled out of the garage, I texted my mom that I would be in New York with Valerie for the weekend. With my parents handled, I set out to make the fifteen-minute drive to the address Christopher had given me right before I left work.

The small cabin was located on the lake, not too far away from his home, and was nestled in a private wooded area. As I pulled up, I found that the two-car garage door had been left open on one side. That meant Christopher had beaten me there. I pulled in, grabbed my bag, and then closed the garage door before heading up to the front of the small log home.

The front door opened, and there stood Christopher, wearing nothing but a towel around his waist. "Hey, baby, you're home!" He held out his arms and I ran into them. "I just got out of the shower and heard you drive up. The door was locked, that's why I'm wearing this towel."

I didn't really care why he wore the fluffy white towel—all I cared about was wrapping myself around the man. "Well, let's get inside and get that thing off you." I wrapped my arms around his neck and he picked me up, carrying me inside.

Barely noticing our surroundings, I gazed into his hazel eyes as I ran my hand through his dark hair. As he walked past the sofa, I tossed my bag onto it. "Wanna see our bedroom?" he asked.

"I do." I giggled at the thought. *Our bedroom.*

He kicked open the door that was just off the living room and took me into what would become our bedroom. "I had this delivered today. I hope you like it."

Looking at the big bed sitting in the middle of the room, I said, "What's not to like?"

Laughing, he tossed me onto the bed, making the pale green blanket fly up on either side of me. "That's what I thought too." He opened his arms to encompass the entire room. "Welcome to our love nest, baby."

"It's beautiful," I gushed as I looked all around the bedroom. Dark green curtains covered the windows, and a ceiling fan stirred the air over the bed.

"I'm going to cook us some steaks on the grill in the backyard. It's pretty secluded out here. No one can see us even from the lake if they pass by on a boat." He leaned down, giving me a sweet little peck on the nose. "I've gotta get the grill started. In the fridge, you'll find everything to make a salad, and I was thinking we could make some baked potatoes, too. You can find them in the pantry."

He turned to walk away from me, letting the towel drop before picking up a pair of shorts off the dresser and slipping into them, and partially dressed, he walked out the bedroom door.

It wasn't the way I thought our weekend would start, but I guessed he wanted me to treat the place like our home—to play husband and wife or something like that. So, I slipped off my shoes and traded my jeans for a pair of shorts before going out to find the kitchen.

He'd put some music on the stereo, and it played softly through the screen door. I danced a little as I found the potatoes and put them in the oven.

Christopher poked his head inside, grinning at me. "Wrap those in aluminum, baby. And make sure the oven's on four-twenty-five, okay?"

Pulling them back out, I looked for the foil after turning up the temperature on the oven. "You got it, boss."

He pushed the screen door open and came inside. Pulling me to him, he put his arms around me then kissed the tip of my nose. "Not boss. Come up with some other nickname or something sweet for me, baby."

"Um—I don't really know what to call you." I felt a little awkward for not knowing what to say—an affectionate nickname should be easy to come by, shouldn't it?

"Think about it." He kissed my cheek then nuzzled my neck.

I thought about the way he made me feel—all warm and sexy. "What if I call you sexy?"

His grin told me he liked that very much. "You can call me that. But only if you really mean it."

Trailing fingers over his bare chest, I let him know exactly what I thought of him. "Christopher, you are the sexiest man I've ever met. Of course I mean it. Now get your sexy ass out there and make me some steak that I may or may not eat."

"Oh, you'll eat it." He let me go then slapped my butt when I turned to get back to my potatoes.

He'd stunned me with the smack, but I was even more stunned by how much I'd liked it. "I will, huh?"

"Yeah, you will. After the way you sucked on my dick, I don't think rare meat will be quite as bad as you thought it would be." He walked out the screen door, leaving me blushing like crazy.

"Damn, that man makes me hot." I fanned myself with my hand before going back to the work of wrapping the potatoes in foil.

A short time later, he came in with a platter of some juicy-looking steaks in one hand and a cold beer in the other. "Mine's ready. How about yours?"

Putting the salad on the small table in the dining nook, I couldn't help the smile that seemed to be glued to my face. "I've got mine ready, too, sexy."

He put the platter down, then went to get some steak sauce and a couple of beers out of the fridge. "Steak and beer—the perfect pairing." He placed them on the table as I put the other things down, too, and then he grabbed me and sat me on his lap, giving me a kiss that had me thinking more about the bedroom than about food. When the kiss ended, he rested his forehead against mine. "Just like me and you, baby. I have a feeling that our weekends are going to be better than any we've ever had."

"I think so too," I whispered, still trying to regain my breath from that devastating kiss.

Before I knew what he was doing, he'd picked me up and sat me down in the chair beside his. "Okay, we don't want the meat to get cold." He stabbed the steak on top then put it on the plate in front of me. "This one is yours. I made sure to trim off all the fat for you."

"That's was nice of you." I looked at the charred surface and thought it looked cooked enough for me. But when I cut into it and some red liquid ran out onto the plate, I looked up to find him smiling at me. "I don't know about this."

He leaned over, cut a nice sized chunk off, and then held the fork near my lips. "Open up."

After taking a deep breath, I closed my eyes and did as I was told. The warm meat melted on my tongue and left me moaning. "More."

When I opened my eyes, he'd leaned back in his seat. "I think you can feed yourself now. I'd like to eat mine while it's warm too."

Sitting like that, just eating at the table like a real couple, I felt happier than I could ever remember. "This is nice."

"I agree." He leaned over to peck my cheek. "Eat up. I want you to have lots of strength for the night I've got planned for you, my sweet little virgin."

Oh, hell!

CHAPTER 17

Christopher

Wanting things to feel nice and normal, the dinner we'd made set the tone. After eating, we washed the dishes side by side, her washing, me drying. As boring a chore as that is, I had to say that I'd never been more entertained.

Emma made me happy just by being near me. "I noticed that you ate every last piece of the steak."

"You were right! What can I say?" she said with a shrug.

"I guess that shows you can trust me even more now." I nudged her with my shoulder, feeling some heat rising up inside of me.

She stopped what she'd been doing to look at me with serious eyes. "Christopher, I trust you completely. That was never in question."

"Good." I pecked her cheek. "You should. I wouldn't ever hurt you, Emma."

"I believe you." She smiled at me then added, "I wouldn't do anything to hurt you either."

"I believe you, too." I took the last dish from her and wiped it with the towel before placing it on the rack. "Now it's time to wash you up, my little love snack."

Giggling as I picked her up bridal style, she wrapped her arms around my neck. "Love snack?"

Nodding, I kissed her neck then nipped it playfully. "Yummy."

A nice hot bubble bath for the two of us should loosen her up. I started the water and then poured in the bubbles as she slipped out of her clothes. Dropping my shorts, I got into the old, claw-footed bathtub before she did, and then took her hand to help her settle in front of me.

With her back to me, I ran my hands over her narrow shoulders then kissed one of them before pulling her back to lie on me. "Here you go, just lay back here and let me run my hands all over you."

She moaned quietly as I moved my hands over her, concentrating on her big tits and playing with the nipples a little before moving down to her stomach. I avoided her pubic area, saving that for last. "God, Christopher, you know how to treat a woman."

Nibbling her earlobe, I whispered, "I know how to treat you, that's for sure."

Every part of her body was beautiful: the way her hips curved; the way her stomach wasn't completely flat, but a little plump; the way her thighs were thick and luscious—everything combined to make her perfect in my eyes.

I knew if it weren't for the fact that there were so many people in our way, then we would already be together by now—truly together. I wouldn't have hesitated to have our relationship be out in the open.

But that wasn't the case. So we'd just have to make sure we made the most of our weekends. Our secret love affair. In the short time I'd known her, my feelings for Emma had already gone a long way to making me feel whole again. And I hoped our relationship would help Emma with her self-esteem and confidence, too.

She began to run her hands up and down my legs. I shiver went down my spine as she turned over, pressing her tits against my chest. Our mouths collided with a passionate kiss. My cock ached for her, but I still didn't want to rush anything.

But it seemed that Emma had different plans. She moved her legs to straddle me, and after lining me up with her already wet pussy, she slid down onto my erection without any hesitation. Her tight canal felt so incredible around me that I held my breath as we kissed.

The tip of my dick hit a wall, or more accurately, her hymen. She wasted no time, pushing down so that my cock broke through it. Whimpering, she took her mouth away from mine. "Oh, that burns." A tear rolled down her cheek, and I ran my thumb over it.

To be honest, I felt some pain, too, as her virgin cunt clamped down on my dick. But the pain was pleasant, even arousing. "It'll get better." I put my hands on her waist to lift her up.

She placed her hands on my shoulders and looked into my eyes as I moved her body to stroke me. "I guess I should've waited for you to make this move, huh?"

"Nah, I like that you did it." I eased her hips back down, watching her eyes close as she began to feel more pleasure than pain. "Better?"

"Um, hmm," she moaned then opened her eyes to look at me again. "You can move me faster if you'd like."

I moved her a little faster, not much. I liked looking at her body as I moved her up and down slowly. Her boobs jiggled slightly with the movement. Leaning up, I took one into my mouth, sucking it gently.

Emma's groan, low and sexy, made me hungrier than ever for a taste of her. Without meaning to, I got more aggressive, moving her faster as I bit and sucked her tit harder.

"Yes! Christopher!" she cried out.

She liked it rough, it seemed, and so did I. Even though I'd never once been rough with my ex-wife, I loved the adrenaline that rushed through my body at the thought of taking that step with Emma. Pulling my mouth away from her succulent tit, I said, "Let's go to our bed and see what we can come up with."

A slow, sexy smile curled her pink lips. "Yeah, let's do that. I can't believe how amazing this feels."

"It only gets better, baby." I picked her all the way up, lifting her off my engorged cock.

She got out of the tub and grabbed a towel to dry off with as I followed suit. Tossing her towel to me, she walked out of the bathroom to get into the bed.

Feeling like some young stud, I barely ran the towel over my body before running after her, and then picking her up and tossing her over my shoulder. I gave her ass a nice slap then took her to our bed. *Our bed!*

Emma's reactions so far couldn't have been a bigger surprise. Starting out shy and innocent and then impaling herself on my erection like that? Wow, who would've seen that coming?

Not that I was complaining. Everything this woman did just seemed to turn me on more.

Tossing her onto the bed, I gazed at her beautiful body. "I've got to say that you've impressed me, baby."

"How's that?" she asked as she looked me over then wiggled her finger in a come-hither gesture. "Come here and tell me about it while you take me like you own me, sexy."

"Holy fuck!" I muttered as I climbed in between her spread legs, ramming my cock into her soft, hot pussy. "You're hot as hell, Emma."

Grunting slightly at the impact of my hard thrust, she said, "So are you, Christopher. Now, show me what I've been missing."

I could see she was eager to know how it felt to be fucked every which way imaginable. I would need to purchase a copy of the Kama Sutra. We'd both learn a few things from that.

My marriage hadn't taught me much more about sex than what I'd already known prior to meeting Lisa. It looked to me like being with Emma would teach me plenty.

I took her hands, pulling them up above her head, and then pinning them to the mattress as I pounded her sweet cunt. Her expression of unadulterated lust made me insane for her. "You like this?"

"How you fuck me?" she asked with a sexy grin. "I like it more than I ever thought I would."

It had been forever since a woman had said anything like that to me—it would've been pre-Lisa, back in my wilder years. Emma took me back to a time when I was in my prime. She made me feel primal, young, virile, and I never wanted that feeling to go away again.

And watching her become more comfortable in her sexuality was one powerful aphrodisiac.

Laying on top of her, I kissed her hard, demanding more from her. She arched up to meet every hard thrust, wanting it more than I ever imagined the young virgin could.

Her legs wrapped around me as she pulled herself up, wanting to feel me even deeper inside of her. I let go of her hands so I could run mine around the backs of her knees, pulling them up and unwrapping her legs from around my body. I spread her further, pinning her knees to the bed, making it possible to go deeper into her sweet pussy.

She groaned as her untried pussy stretched even more for me. "You're a perfect fit for me, baby."

Through gritted teeth, she gasped, "Only you, my sexy man."

My cock strained, wanting to release, but I wanted to come with her. I'd never cared about that before. But I wanted to give Emma more than I'd ever given anyone, including the woman I'd married.

I should've known by now that Emma was full of surprises, but her next words shocked me so much that I stopped moving. "Spank me and take me from behind," she whispered.

I had never done anything like that before. "Are you sure?" I had to ask.

She nodded as I looked down at her. "Pull my hair, go crazy on me."

The idea set me on fire. I pulled out of her and then flipped her over onto her stomach. Leaving her lying on the bed, I raised my hand then let it fall onto her ass cheek with a loud smack. I saw my handprint on her creamy ass and smacked it again.

Over and over, I spanked her until her whole ass was red. She whimpered and mewled, even cried out a few times, but she never asked me to stop. When she started pushing her hips back toward me —as if to increase the contact between my hand and her ass—I couldn't take it anymore. I pushed her legs apart and laid down on top of her back, pushing my erection into her pulsing pussy.

Biting her neck, I held her flesh between my teeth as I growled, "That should teach you not to be bad, baby." I grabbed a handful of her silky hair, yanking it back to expose more of her neck. I took a bigger bite of hot flesh as I fucked her relentlessly.

Moving her body back on forth on the bed with every hard thrust, I knew her clit was being stimulated like crazy, and I couldn't wait to feel her come around my aching cock.

She mewed and purred as I fucked her, "Christopher…sexy…oh, my God!"

The way her already tight canal started to tighten around my dick made me growl like an animal. It pulsed and squeezed, and I made some terrible sounds as her orgasm tortured me in the most exquisite way. "Baby! Ah!" I burst inside her like never before. "Fuck!"

I couldn't hear a thing except for our combined groans, moans, and the way we both panted like we'd run a hundred miles.

Unable to move, I lay on top of her, trying to catch my breath. When my head cleared a little, I worried I might be squishing her. Rolling off, I fell to one side of her. Then she rolled onto her back. "Better than I ever imagined."

I laughed a little. "Yeah, for me too."

Emma moved around to lay her head on my chest. "You've spoiled me for other men, you know."

I wrapped my arm around her and kissed the top of her head. "I hope so."

It wasn't fair, and I knew that. Emma deserved more than a secret love affair. She deserved to have a normal relationship like anyone else. But she'd chosen to give herself to me. And as selfish as it was, I wasn't about to give her any freedom to see anyone else, so long as she was with me.

Her fingertips trailed over my chest as her soft lips pressed against my skin. "I don't think I'll ever get tired of this."

"Me neither." I squeezed her and told her what I'd been thinking. "I don't want you to see anyone else, Emma."

She lifted her head to look at me. At first, she seemed confused, but then a smile took over. "Did you think I'd have one taste of sex with you and then go wild, wanting to have sex with any man around, Christopher?"

I didn't know what I thought. I only thought that I wanted her to be with me and only me. "No. I just wanted to put it out there."

She put her head back down on my chest. "No need to worry, sexy. I only want you anyway."

Good.

CHAPTER 18

Emma

Our first weekend together had taught me a lot. Some of it I already had an inkling about, like I really liked spending time with Christopher. Others were a bit more of a surprise, like I really, really liked having sex with him! Like, couldn't get enough of him.

The next weekend was more of the same. On the way home from our second weekend together, I called Valerie to tell her how great things were going. "So, I'm leaving to go home now. I just wanted to let you know."

"Thank you," Val said appreciatively. "So, how's it all going?"

I didn't know where to start, but ventured forward anyway. "Well, he's fantastic. And I'm having the best time of my life."

"Naturally." She snickered. "First love is always the best time of your life. And then it fades away, and life gets in the way." With a barely suppressed laugh, she continued, "I just want you to know that this will end, is what I'm trying to say, Emma."

I didn't want to think about it ending, even if she was joking. "Shut up!"

"Jokes aside, there is some truth to that," she went on. "It's all hot and heavy in the beginning, and then the newness tends to wear off. I'm not saying you two will break up. I'm just saying that this euphoric ride you're both on will likely slow down a hell of a lot. I don't want you to be blindsided if that happens."

I could tell she was trying to be a good friend, but I didn't want to think about the future; I wanted to continue being happy with what we had. "Thanks for the kind words, dear friend, but I think for the next little bit, it'll continue to be a euphoric ride."

"Yeah, for the next little bit," she sighed. "So, this is your second weekend together. When do you think you're going to let your parents know about your man, Emma?"

Never.

I still hadn't told her about the age difference or that Christopher was Dad's friend and our boss. I didn't think she needed to know all that. No—scratch that—I didn't want to hear what she'd say about it. I knew she'd tell me it was a bad idea and that I should call it all off. And I didn't want to hear that.

"You know how my parents are, Valerie." I turned onto our street and had to wrap up the call. "For now, we're not telling anyone about us."

"Tell me his name," she pushed. "That way if anything happens to you, at least I'll know who you've been with."

"That would be the safest and smartest thing to do." I knew that. But I knew I couldn't tell her his name. "And maybe I'll tell you sometime, but not today. I've just pulled up at the house, and Mom's already heading out here to greet me," I lied.

"Fine, but I'll get his name out of you eventually! Talk to you later," she said before ending the call.

Laughing at her determination, I parked the car in the garage then grabbed my bag and got out. My body still tingled from Christopher's touch. Our parting kiss still felt fresh on my lips.

I wished we could talk on the phone, but he said that would be too risky. The days I'd seen him at work the past week, it'd been hard to keep myself from touching him, kissing him, wrapping my arms around him. But the thought of the weekend to come had helped me through it.

Already, I counted the days until he and I could sleep in the same bed, holding each other through the night. Each morning we'd been together he'd woken me up with a kiss that had quickly turned into so much more. Most morning we hadn't gotten out of bed until just before noon, our stomachs growling for us to get up and make breakfast together.

Only two weekends in and already I craved that lifestyle every single day and night.

Walking into the house, I heard Mom and Dad in the main living area. "That you, honey?" Mom called out.

"Yes, Mom." I tossed my bag on the bottom stair before going in to see them.

They had some movie playing on the television, and Dad paused it. "So, how was your visit with Valerie this weekend?"

"Good. We just hung around her apartment and watched movies. It was okay." I shrugged. "You know, something to do."

Dad nodded. "Well, next weekend we don't want you to make any plans."

My heart stopped. *I can't not see Christopher!* "Why?"

Mom chimed in, "It's our anniversary, sweetie. You know we always go on a little trip. We're planning on heading up to Canada to do some fishing. Won't that be fun?"

I'd always gone on their anniversary trips with them. And we always had fun. But I didn't want to have that kind of fun anymore. "Val and I already made plans; I totally forgot about your anniversary. I'm sorry, but I'm not going to make it for this one."

Dad's face told me he wasn't going to let it go that easily. "Cancel your plans, Emma. We've already booked a two-bedroom cabin. You're coming with us."

Not used to telling my father no, I didn't know what to say. My shoulders sagged, feeling helpless.

Mom got up and came to put her arm around me. "Don't look so blue, sweetie. We're going to have fun just like we always do."

"But Val's going to be so disappointed." I knew Christopher would be disappointed and so would I, but Val was the only name I could say out loud.

"She'll get over it," Dad said.

Then Mom got a bright idea. "I know, let's invite Valerie too."

"No," I said quickly.

Dad looked at me with an odd expression. "And why not?"

"She won't want to go. She hates outdoor stuff." I didn't know what to say, but that came out of my mouth so quickly. It seemed I could lie pretty easily.

Mom patted me on the back. "Let her know that you won't be joining her next weekend. We'll have a nice time, you'll see. I want to get back to this movie and finish it before I fall asleep. And you've got work to get up early for. It's nearly eleven now. You came in later than you did last Sunday night."

It was much harder to pull myself away from Christopher this time.

Heading back to the stairs, I picked up my bag off the step then went up to my bedroom. My only hope was that Christopher would help me figure out a way to get out of this.

The next morning I hurried to work, only to find Christopher hadn't come in yet. Then around eleven o'clock, Mrs. Kramer told me that he'd gone to meet the men from China in Concord. I'd forgotten all about that meeting.

He would be bringing them back for the meeting sometime after lunch. That meant he'd be busy with them all day and even into the evening. We'd never get a chance to talk.

Suddenly, I hated the fact that we couldn't talk in the open. That I couldn't pick up the phone and call him.

"Where's Daddy?" I heard a woman say as I stepped out into the hallway.

Mrs. Kramer stood in front of Christopher's office door as two tall, willowy blondes dressed to the nines stood in front of her. "He's with some clients. He'll be busy all day. Tomorrow the clients will be leaving, and he can see you two after that. I don't want you girls to bother him today—or tomorrow morning either."

One of them rolled her eyes. "We haven't seen him in days, since he went out of town this weekend. He came in so late last night and left so early this morning that we didn't get to talk to him. And we wanted to talk to him about a surprise we want to give our mother. We need his approval for it."

Jealousy spiked through me at the thought that he would have anything to do with a surprise for his ex-wife. But Mrs. Kramer quickly put their idea to rest. "If it has to do with your mother and him, I can tell you what he'll say."

"I know." The shorter of the two nearly identical girls said. "But Mom really wants to spend the Fourth of July weekend at our lake house, and that's next weekend."

I hadn't even realized this coming weekend was the holiday. And with me having to go with Mom and Dad, what if Christopher did end up spending the weekend with his daughters and ex-wife?

Mrs. Kramer gave a quick reply, "That lake house is your father's home. And you both know very well that he does not want your mother there. Now, why are you two trying to make them spend time together when you know what happened between them? Your father was very hurt by what your mother did. I thought you loved your father and understood this."

"She won't stop bothering us about it, Mrs. Kramer," the taller of the two confessed.

"Then I'll give her a call," Mrs. Kramer said. "After all she's done to him, I'm not going to allow her to bother him. You two run along now. I've got work to get to." Mrs. Kramer turned and found me standing just outside my office door. "Miss Hancock, there you are. I need you to get the conference room ready. Hurry now."

I rushed passed the three women, Christopher's daughters not even bothering to glance my way, which made me feel oddly insignificant. I immediately understood why he worried about his daughters finding out about us—there's no way in the world that he and I could have a relationship that those two were aware of.

As I hurried to get the conference room ready, I stopped a moment to look out the window. I saw Christopher walking up the sidewalk, his daughters meeting him halfway. He hugged them both, then shook his head as they said something to him.

Those girls had asked him about their mother coming for the weekend anyway!

I just knew they had. I could tell by his reaction and the stern look on his handsome face.

The men I'd expected to see with him were nowhere to be seen, so I hauled ass to see if I could speak with Christopher if only for a second. Heading down to the main floor in his private elevator, I knew that would be the best way to get a tiny bit of alone time with the man.

When I got to the lobby, the doors opened and Christopher stepped onto the elevator with his head down, not noticing me. He pushed the button to our floor. "Hi there," I finally said, grabbing his attention.

He spun around then frowned at me. "Emma!"

"I've just gotta say this really quick. My parents are making me go to Canada this weekend for their anniversary trip. I don't know what to do." I wanted to reach out and touch him but didn't dare.

The way his eyes drooped told me he'd had a bad day already and that this wasn't helping. "Damn."

"Are you okay?" I asked, and then I looked at the numbers as they flashed with each floor we passed. Our time was running out.

"I'll be fine. The Chinese merchants want a different deal than we'd planned. And my ex-wife is trying to weasel her way into my home. And now this." He stepped toward me and pulled me into his arms. "God, I need you, baby."

My heart hurt so much as he held onto me. The ding of the elevator had us jumping apart. We'd reached the top floor. "Maybe we can meet at our place after work?"

"I'll be too busy trying to close this deal with them." He looked at the doors as they opened. "Fuck it. Meet me there around ten. Tell your parents you're going to Concord to pick up some things our guests left behind, and that we've set you up to stay the night there."

Then he walked out, leaving me there as the doors closed on me once more.

I felt as if I were in the middle of a whirlwind. My head was a little out of it, wondering what had just happened, but I was also elated that I would get to spend the night with my sexy man again.

But what about the weekend?

CHAPTER 19

Christopher

The problems kept stacking up. I had to think about how to get Emma out of the trip with her parents, when all I really needed to be thinking about was how to solve the difference of opinions between myself and my potential clients.

"We're talking about a few cents, guys," I told the gentlemen, who wouldn't budge a penny on their offer.

Sebastien showed up, coming in only a couple of minutes late. "Sorry, everyone. I got tied up." He took the seat at the other end of the table, and I let him have the floor. I was tired of trying to get the men to understand my reasoning.

"I'm going to take a break. I'll be back in a little while, Sebastien." I left the room, feeling worn out.

I had a stack of problems in front of me and no idea how to handle any of them—except for the issue of my ex-wife wanting to come to my home for the holiday weekend. That one was easy. I'd told my daughters that they could tell their mother it would *never* happen.

The four-day weekend had crept up on me. That could be

attributed to Emma; my mind had been occupied with nothing but thoughts of her for the past two weeks. All I wanted to do was spend that long weekend with her, but it seemed that wasn't going to be as easy I wanted it to be.

If Emma and I could've just been honest about our relationship, then this wouldn't have been a problem. But since we couldn't, it felt like an enormous issue.

I supposed it wouldn't have seemed like a big deal to most people. *So what if I couldn't spend the holiday with Emma; it's only one weekend, right?*

The thing was I'd had a hard enough time letting her go just the night before. Knowing I would have her back in my arms in only four days was the only thing that got me through it. If I couldn't see her that weekend, it would be eleven days before I got to hold her, kiss her, make love to her again.

I just couldn't hold out for that long. And by the desperation in her voice and expression when she'd surprised me on the elevator, Emma didn't think she could hold out that long either. Funny how a couple of weekends together could make us so needy for each other.

Going into my office, I sat at my desk and opened my laptop. Whenever my own brain wasn't working as it should, I always turned to the web. When I searched, 'great excuses to get out of plans,' the first excuse on the list I'd found was to fake illness.

I thought about that for a second. Emma could tell her parents she felt sick or had a stomach bug and didn't want to ruin their trip by getting everyone sick.

The idea sounded great until I really thought about it. Her parents would most likely put their trip off and stay home with her. And that would still mean she wouldn't be able to spend the weekend with me.

Onto the next idea. The old, 'my boss is making me work' excuse. Another one that just wouldn't work for us, since I was her father's friend, and I would never pull rank on his family outing.

Then there were a bunch of other excuses that wouldn't work: 'I've gotta clean my house;' 'I've sprained my ankle;' 'I've got personal family issues;' 'Car trouble;' and the best one I'd ever heard: 'I'm ovulating and we're trying for a baby.'

So, no luck there. I sat staring at the screen, trying to come up with anything better than the garbage I'd just read, when there was a knock at my door. Closing the laptop, I called out, "Come in."

Sebastien strode in like some kind of a hero, swaggering with each step. The smile on his face told it all. "So, I've come to an agreement with our new clients, Christopher." He came to my desk, placing the signed contract on it. "And we didn't lose a cent." With his chest puffed up with great pride, he took a seat in the chair opposite me.

I didn't care how he'd accomplished it, I was just happy he'd done it. "Well, congratulations, my good man." I got up and went to pat him on the back then poured us a couple of glasses of my good Scotch. And as I did that, an idea formed in my brain. "Don't you and Celeste have an anniversary coming up?"

"We do. It's this weekend." Sebastien took the glass I offered him. "Thank you."

As he took a sip, I came up with a plan on the fly. "As a token of my appreciation for this job well done, I would like to offer you and your lovely wife a five night, six-day anniversary trip to Bora Bora."

He looked properly stunned. "When?"

"Well, for your anniversary of course." I retook my seat then sipped the Scotch.

"But we've already made plans to go to Canada. Celeste rented a cabin, and we were going to go fishing." He took another drink as he seemed to rethink things.

I could see I needed to sweeten the already sweet deal. "Of course, there's also the big bonus you're getting for bringing me a signed contract—you'll probably want to celebrate that, too."

Taking out my pen, I jotted down a very nice number on a piece of paper then slid it to him. He picked it up, looking at it with wide eyes. "Is this the amount of the bonus?"

"It is." I opened the laptop to send an e-mail to Mrs. Kramer. "My assistant will have that amount deposited into your bank account by tomorrow morning. That should help you and Celeste have a nice time on your little anniversary vacation. I expect she'll be pleasantly surprised that you two will be having a little fun in the sun, instead of fighting off bears in the Canadian wilderness."

"Yeah, she'll be surprised alright." He took his eyes off the paper and then shook his head as he looked at me. "But Emma."

I held up my hand. "She'll be fine, Sebastien. Go have a nice anniversary with your wife. Taking your daughter with you everywhere you go has to have been cramping the romance in your marriage all these years?"

He nodded. "A little, yeah. But Celeste won't want to leave Emma here all alone for such a long time."

"Convince her to." I took another drink of my Scotch, feeling like I'd just cured cancer or something for coming up with this plan.

Not only would I get to spend the weekend with Emma, but I'd have her for nearly an entire week if I could pull this off. My nether regions were already getting excited, but I sternly cleared my mind of those thoughts, not wanting my friend to be aware of any of that.

Sebastien slapped his hand on my desk. "I'll convince her! This is by far the coolest thing anyone has ever done for me, Christopher."

"Hey, you've earned this, ol' boy. I didn't give you anything." I got up and shook his hand. "You've just made this company millions, maybe even billions, Sebastien!"

"Yeah, I have, haven't I?" He got up as well and started making his way to the office door. "I'm going to my office to call Celeste now and tell her the great news. And I'm sure Emma will be happy for us. Plus, you'll be here to help her if anything happens, right?"

"I will." I walked with him to the door then opened it. "She'll be in good hands here. You two just go and have a great time. I'll have Mrs. Kramer e-mail you the details about the trip, the flight, and everything else you'll need."

While Sebastien went to his office, I headed to my assistant's office. Opening the door, I found Mrs. Kramer talking to Emma. "I need you to make some arrangements, Mrs. Kramer." I nodded at Emma. "How are you doing today, Miss Hancock?"

"Just fine, sir." Emma smiled as she ducked her head, looking shy.

"Good to hear." I turned my attention to my assistant. "Have you checked your e-mail yet? I've just sent you something."

"No, sir." Mrs. Kramer looked at Emma. "Can you do that for me?"

Emma sat at the desk, pulling up the e-mail. I knew the moment she opened it, as she smiled knowingly. "Seems my father's earned a nice bonus." Emma turned the computer around for Mrs. Kramer to see.

"Oh, I need to get that done fairly quickly then." Mrs. Kramer took the seat that Emma had vacated.

"And I want you to make Mr. Hancock and his wife reservations at one of the resorts in Bora Bora. Get them everything. The plane, the hotel, the whole thing. I want them to leave on Thursday, and they'll be spending five nights there. Okay?"

"I'll do it. I'll e-mail everything to Mr. Hancock as soon as I get it all done, Mr. Taylor." Mrs. Kramer got right to work as Emma stared at me with a shocked expression.

"Your father got the contract signed, Miss Hancock. He's earned this reward," I informed her. "We treat our people very well here."

"You sure do," she said quietly.

Knowing that Mrs. Kramer was unaware of everything but the task in front of her, I winked at Emma. "I'll be leaving around three today. I'm going to need you to leave around then too. It seems one of our guests left something behind at the hotel in Concord, and it needs to be retrieved before they leave tomorrow morning. I'll need you to get it, Miss Hancock. I'll let your father know that you'll be out of town for the night and that he'll see you here tomorrow morning."

"'Kay," she said, still stunned. "I'll leave at three to go to Concord."

"Have a good trip," I said before leaving. "Drive carefully."

A couple of hours later, I wasn't surprised at all when Emma strolled into our cabin with a grin that wouldn't quit on her face. "So, am I to expect that you and I will be spending our nights here while my parents are away?"

"Not just the nights, Miss Hancock." I pulled her into my arms then kissed her sweet lips before telling her the good news. "You've got the same days off that I gave your father. This Thursday all the way through to next Tuesday. Do you think you can stand spending that much time with me in our little love nest, baby?"

The way she wrapped her body around mine told me she thought she could handle that. "I must warn you, sexy, you're spoiling me terribly."

I can think of worse things.

CHAPTER 20

Emma

Two months went by with me and Christopher spending as much time together as we could steal at the cabin. Another Monday had come where I'd had to pull myself away from the man at nearly two in the morning to go back to my parents' house.

The day hit me hard and heavy as my alarm went off. Staggering to my bathroom, I felt a knot in my stomach that made me nauseous. I held my stomach as I went to the sink to brush my teeth.

In a sudden wave of heat and dizziness, I changed directions, heading to the toilet instead where I puked my very soul up. I felt so weak I had to sit on the cold tile floor. "What the hell?" I whimpered.

After a few minutes I managed to heave my body up and went right back to bed, lying down and trying to figure out what I'd eaten or drank to suddenly be feeling so terrible.

Christopher and I had made spaghetti for dinner Sunday night. I'd had one glass of wine with that, certainly not enough to make me feel this sick.

Rolling onto my side, I closed my eyes, which felt like they were burning for some reason. When I opened them, I found ten minutes had passed. I got out of bed and went to get into the shower to wake myself up and hope that it would make me feel better.

The cool water did bring me around. My head felt better, and after toweling off and giving my teeth a good brushing, I felt more alive and able to take on the workday.

I needed to get a fresh hand towel from underneath the sink, and I reached down to grab one. That's when my attention was caught by an unopened box of tampons.

...the same box of tampons I'd bought to replace the one I'd used up during my last period. Two months ago.

Leaning over, I said the words out loud. "Two. Months. Ago."

Two months ago?

Standing up straight, I looked at myself in the mirror. "Emma Eileen Hancock, you did not do this to yourself!"

In a daze, I went back to my bed to sit down before I fell down. It all came flooding back to me. Each and every time Christopher and I had made love flashed in my head—and then the most significant thing illuminated in my brain, burning a hole in it. *Birth control.*

I'd never gotten on it. I'd never talked about it with Christopher either. We'd never used protection a single time in the last two months. And now I'd missed a period.

I picked my cell up off the nightstand and looked at my notes. I hadn't missed just one period; I'd missed two of them. I should've had one the week before.

I had to get a test. A test would prove what I already knew, but I wouldn't let myself actually think it until I had the proof in my hands.

On the way to work, I stopped by a drugstore to pick up a pregnancy test. Hiding it in my purse, I took it in with me when I got in my office, heading straight to my private bathroom.

Peeing on a stick wasn't exactly the way I thought I'd start my workday when I went to bed last night, but then again, I hadn't thought I'd wake up puking either.

Minutes later, I stared at the line that told me that I'd fucked up my life royally. And Christopher's too, for that matter.

I couldn't get out of there fast enough. Grabbing my purse, I bolted out of my office, heading down the long hallway to the stairwell. I wasn't about to use the elevator and chance running into anyone.

After three flights of stairs, I had to sit down on a step and catch my breath. My head spun from lack of oxygen and the fact that I'd been so damn stupid. "You're truly an idiot, Emma Hancock."

I sat there, not sure what I should do. Only one thought came to me. *Valerie.*

Getting up, I took the stairs at a slower pace so I wouldn't pass out and break my neck by falling down the stairs. *But then again, that might not be so bad.*

It took forever, but I finally made it to the ground floor. I had to get to my car in the parking garage without anyone seeing me and asking why I was leaving.

Remarkably, I made it out and slipped into my car. My hands shook as I clutched the steering wheel. I had to get to Valerie; she'd know what to do. At least I hoped she would.

In my panic, I hadn't even called her; I just drove like a bat out of hell. Pulling up at the dorms at Columbia, I got out of my car and went to her dorm room, only to find that no one was there.

After knocking for five minutes, I leaned my back against the door and then slowly slid down the wall. Now it was officially time to break down. "No!" I cried as I put my face in my hands and started bawling.

"What are you doing, Emma?" came a girl's voice.

I looked up but couldn't see through my tears. "Val?"

"Of course it's me. No one else knows you here, Emma." She reached down to help me up. "What happened? Did Romeo break up with you or something?"

"No," I wailed.

"Did someone run over your dog?" she asked sarcastically.

"No," I cried.

"Let's go inside. People are coming, and they'll call security on your loud ass." She unlocked the door then pulled me inside, taking me to her bed and making me sit down. "I'm going to get a wet washcloth to clean your teary face, then you're going to stop bawling and tell me what the hell is wrong."

Gasping as I tried to stop crying, I kept wiping away the tears that refused to stop falling. When Valerie came back with the cool, wet cloth, I took it from her and held it to my burning eyes until I was able to stop the tears, and I felt like I might be able to say the words I needed to.

"I... I..." I couldn't do it. I fell apart again and fell on the bed, burying my face in the pillow.

"Emma! For the love of God. Please pull yourself together," she pleaded with me. "Plus, that's my roommate's pillow you're covering in your snot and tears. That's gross, man!"

"Sorry," I mumbled as I put the cloth over my eyes again to try to stop the flood of tears a second time, but it didn't work.

Nothing would work. I would most likely die of dehydration at the rate I was going. And everyone would be better off that way, anyway.

I could never go to Christopher with this horrible news. I couldn't tell my parents, either. I didn't know what I would do.

Valerie lay on the bed beside me, holding me in her thin arms. "Just try to calm down, Emma. Nothing is this bad. We can deal with whatever's wrong. You'll see. Hush, now. No more crying. Crying has never solved anything."

I knew she was right. But nothing would solve my problem.

At least I had money in my bank account for once in my life. I could run away and start a new life under an assumed name. Maybe Connie Beavers or something like that. I would have my baby and raise it all on my own. Even though I didn't know a single thing about babies or about being a mom.

The thought made me cry even harder. "Valerie, I've messed up. I've messed up real bad!"

"How?" she asked as she rubbed my shoulders. "Come on, Emma, tell me what's wrong. This is killing me. I'm serious."

"I can't." A whole new level of crying started. Deep, guttural, as if my soul itself was being torn apart.

"Damn it!" she yelled at me as she got off the bed. "Sit up and tell me what the hell's happened! Right now, young lady!"

Her tone shocked me, and I sat up, wiping my eyes. "You can't tell anyone, Val. I mean it. Not anyone."

"What did this asshole do to you, Emma?" She smacked her fist against her palm. "I'm going to kill him!"

"It's not his fault." I tried to catch my breath and hold the tears back. "It's all mine."

"I'm sure it's his fault." She paced back and forth. "I should've never kept your secret. Now this jerk has gone and done something terrible to you, and it's all my fault. I should've told you to tell your parents about him. I should've made you let me meet him. There're so many things I should've done. You're too naïve. Too trusting. Too innocent. This is all my fault, Emma." She began to cry too as she fell on her knees in front of me, taking my hands in hers. "Please forgive me, Emma!"

Now we were both wailing, and I didn't know how to stop it.

The cell in my purse started ringing, and I had to take it out to see who it was. Through a blur of tears, I saw it was Mrs. Kramer. She had to be wondering where the hell I was.

Valerie took the phone out of my hands. "Who's Mrs. Kramer, Emma?"

"Don't answer it." I took the phone back and turned it off. "I can't talk to anyone. I'll break down."

"You've already broken down," she reminded me.

As I stuffed the cell back into my purse, I started to calm down a little. I had to think of what to do. I couldn't just spend the rest of my life sitting in Valerie's dorm room crying my eyes out. That wouldn't be any kind of a life for my baby—the one I didn't know how to take care of in the first place.

"Valerie, I never got on birth control," I finally managed to say.

"Oh," she said then stood up. "That's not a big deal." She wiped her eyes and then straightened out her shirt, which had gotten all out of whack. "I'll take you to the clinic I go to. They allow walk-ins. You don't even have to pay; it's all free."

Somehow, the words wouldn't come out of my mouth. It felt like if I just didn't say them, then it wouldn't be true or something like that. "No."

She shook her head. "No? What does that mean, Emma? Don't you want to get on birth control? I mean, you don't want anyone to know you're dating this guy. If you don't get on birth control, then you'll have to tell everyone that you guys have been screwing around if you get yourself pregnant."

I just stared at her, hoping she wouldn't make me say it. But she seemed kind of clueless. Or maybe she just didn't want to think it either.

Without any idea of what to do, I reached into my purse and pulled out the little stick that had changed my life. Holding it out to her, I closed my eyes so I wouldn't see the disappointment on her face as my reality sank into her brain.

"Oh, no," she whispered. Her arms came around me as she hugged me. "Oh, Emma."

"I've really messed up, Val," I whimpered.

"I know," she whimpered right back. "This is bad, really bad."

So, I hadn't been wrong or overly dramatic. This really was bad. I'd messed up worse than I ever had before. And I hadn't ever really messed up, so my parents would be genuinely shocked and utterly disappointed.

Christopher would hate me. I knew that for sure. He'd hate me for getting pregnant. He'd hate me for leaving him, which I knew I had to. He'd hate me for being so immature as to not get myself on birth control before giving myself to him.

And he'll hate our baby too.

CHAPTER 21

Christopher

"What do you mean she's not answering your calls?" I asked Mrs. Kramer, who seemed genuinely worried about Emma and her whereabouts.

Pacing in front of my desk, she answered, "I've called her ten times now. It's after lunch, and she still hasn't answered my calls. I went to security and saw video of her coming in this morning at a quarter to nine. Not twenty minutes later, she left the building, got in her car in the parking garage and sped off. She looked distraught, Mr. Taylor."

The fact that I was just being told about this now aggravated me. "Why didn't you tell me this sooner?" I got out of my chair, planning to head down the hall to see if Sebastien knew anything about where his daughter might be. "Have you asked her father if he knows where she is?"

"No," she said quietly. "I didn't want to tell him anything in case she didn't want him to know what she was doing. She asked me to keep him out of things where she's concerned. You know how he treats her like a child. Surely you can understand why I didn't go to him about this."

"You could've come to me though," I snapped at her, not meaning to.

She looked a little shocked as she said, "I'm sorry. I didn't think the president of the company would want to be bothered over someone as insignificant as my assistant, sir."

I saw her point and tried to control my anger, knowing it would seem unreasonable in her eyes, particularly if my relationship with Emma were truly as innocent as Mrs. Kramer and everyone else thought it was. "Sorry for snapping at you, Mrs. Kramer. You keep trying to call her. Leave her a few texts asking her to contact you because you're worried about her. I'll go see her father."

We left my office with Mrs. Kramer headed to hers and me headed to Sebastien's. I heard him on the phone just before I knocked. He ended the call then called out, "Come in."

Entering his office, I tried my best not to come across as too worried. "Hey, Sebastien. Mrs. Kramer is worried about Emma. She came to work this morning but then left without telling anyone. And she's not taking Mrs. Kramer's calls either. Do you happen to know if she went home sick or something?"

"She's not home. I was just on the phone with Celeste, and she didn't say anything about Emma being there." He picked up his phone. "But I'll ask her just to be sure."

Taking a seat, I tried to act like I was only vaguely interested in his daughter's disappearance. "I'm sure she's there. Tell her to check her bed and bathroom just to be sure."

"Okay," he said, waiting for the phone to be answered on the other end. "Honey, did Emma go back home this morning?"

"No," I heard Celeste say. "Why?"

"Well, her boss said that Emma was here and then left without telling anyone. Would you go check her room and bathroom, just in case?" he asked his wife.

Waiting to hear what she said, I tried even harder not to show the worry that had begun to gnaw at me. Sebastien shook his head as his wife told him something, and then he looked at me, concern clear in his eyes. "She's not there, Christopher."

Getting up, I knew I needed to go check our cabin to see if she'd gone there for some reason. "Give Emma a call yourself, Sebastien. Maybe she's upset with Mrs. Kramer or something and just doesn't want to talk to her."

"I will." He called her while I waited by the door to see if she answered him. "Emma?"

My heart pounded. *We've found her!*

"Is she okay?" I asked.

He held up one finger. "Honey, stop crying. Tell me where you are."

I couldn't hear a thing she said through the phone, so I walked back toward Sebastian's desk, hoping I could listen in. But before I even got within eavesdropping distance, he put the cell down with a puzzled expression on his face.

"What did she say?" I asked with concern.

"That she's okay—and that she's moving away." He shook his head in disbelief. "And I'm not to worry about her. She's a grown woman who can take care of herself."

"That doesn't make any sense." I spun around to go call her myself, but I wasn't about to let her father know that. "I'll let Mrs. Kramer know that you talked to her."

Going straight to her office, I opened the door to tell Mrs. Kramer the news. I found her on the phone. She waved me in as she spoke to whoever was on the line, "I don't understand, Miss Hancock. Why do you want to quit?"

Emma wants to quit?

Nothing made sense. Emma had left me around two that morning. She'd said nothing about any of the things she was now doing. Something had to have happened to make her do such a rash thing.

My ex-wife popped into my head. *Did she talk to Emma and tell her some kind of lie about me?*

Whatever it was, Emma had to talk to me about it. "Tell her to call me, Mrs. Kramer."

"Miss Hancock, Mr. Taylor wants you to call him." She held out her phone. "Or you can just talk to her now, sir."

Shaking my head, I said, "Tell her to call me. Tell her to do it right now."

"He wants you to call him right now, Miss Hancock," she said. Then she frowned and hung up the phone. "Um— She said no and hung up."

No?

Resisting the urge to storm off the way I wanted to, I shrugged my shoulders and walked away at a reasonable pace, trying not to show any a telling reaction. I kept walking out until I got to my car, which I quickly pointed towards the cabin, all the while trying to get Emma to answer her damn phone.

When I finally arrived at the cabin, I found it empty. She wasn't there, and now I was really worried.

I took out my phone and texted her, asking her to call me and letting her know that I was sick with worry. I prayed she'd at the very least text me back. But she never did.

I knew one thing: Emma had only one friend in this world that she'd turn to if something was wrong. Only one person she trusted: *Valerie*.

The thing was, I didn't even know the girl's last name. I knew she was a student at Columbia in New York, but nothing more than that.

Going to the cabin's bedroom, I found my laptop on the dresser. Emma had been using it to play games and mess around on social media that weekend. I hoped I could open her apps to see if she'd left any clues as to why she would run off that way.

As far as I knew, things were going exceptionally well. Emma and I were as happy as a couple of clams. She never complained about work—not to me at least. And her parents hadn't bugged her about being gone every weekend.

In my opinion, she had nothing to run away from.

But then again, I didn't know if she had any outside influences that might have gotten into her head.

Popping open the computer, I saw that she'd closed all the apps.

Emma was the only one who used the device, so I thought she might've saved the passwords on some of her social media accounts.

One by one, I went through her accounts, and nothing jumped out at me. She'd liked some posts and made a few of her own, but nothing pointed to the reason she'd decided to leave.

I made sure to check the dates and times of the posts, to see if she'd posted anything recently. She hadn't.

I did find out Valerie's last name, and I could send her an instant message. I did—immediately.

Valerie, this is Emma's boyfriend. I need to talk to her ASAP. Please have her call me.

Now all I could do was wait. And wait. And wait.

I fell asleep on the bed as I waited for her to respond or for Emma to call. And the dreams I had were terrible. I'd never had a dramatic imagination, but with Emma's unexpected departure, my brain went crazy.

In my dreams, Emma had been kidnapped by someone, and I couldn't get to her. That morphed into Emma secretly hating me, and she ran away from me to put an end to our relationship. When I woke, I was panting; the dream had spiraled into me chasing her, running after her crying her name.

Checking the instant message box on the computer, I found no reply. In desperation, I typed another.

Valerie, please, please, I am begging you to convince Emma to call me. I've got to know why she left. Was it because of me?

Staring at the screen, I blinked with disbelief as one word appeared. *No.*

I had no idea what that meant, so I typed, *No to what?*

She sent back, *It's not because of you, exactly.*

Then what is it? I sent back.

I got nothing after that. Not a single word came back to me.

What could it mean: *Not because of me, exactly*? Was the girl was playing games with me? And I felt like Emma had to be with her friend, or how else would Valerie know what was going on?

My cell rang, and I jumped off the bed, pulling it out of my pocket and nearly dropping it as my hands shook. The name on the screen wasn't Emma's though. It was my daughter Lauren calling.

"What is it, Lauren?"

"Well, hello to you, too, Daddy," she said with a laugh.

"I'm in the middle of something, sweetheart." I didn't want her to hear the worry I knew threaded through my voice. "What do you need?"

"Nothing, really," she said. "I just wondered what time you'd be coming home and if you and I and Ashley could go out to dinner this evening. I'm bored."

"You could get a job, and then you might not be so bored," I told her.

Her laugh told me she thought I had to be joking. "Daddy, you're so funny. So, really, what time will you be home?"

I had no idea when I'd be home. "You and your sister can go and eat without me. I'll be working late."

"Maybe Mom will want to eat with us," she whined. "You haven't been spending much time with us at all. You're gone every weekend, you know. We hardly ever see you. All we wanted was to go to dinner with you and spend a little time with you."

Guilt over how little time I had spent with my daughters began to set in. "Look, how about we plan it for tomorrow, Lauren?" Surely I would have this thing with Emma straightened out by then.

"Okay, fine. Here's the real reason we wanted to talk to you tonight," she confessed. "There's this little island in the Caribbean that Ashley and I saw on the internet, and it's for sale, Daddy! We want you to buy it for us."

I should've known they wanted something.

"I'm not buying you girls an island." I'd grown more and more aggravated with my daughters the past few months. They really had no aspirations at all, except to spend as much of my money as they possibly could. "But you're right, we do need to talk. Not about what you want me to buy, but about what I want the two of you to start doing. It's time to make some changes. It's time for you and your sister to stop following in your mother's footsteps and take a page out of my book for a change."

"What does that even mean?" she asked, sounding confused.

"I'll get into it much deeper tomorrow night, when you, your sister, and I have a little sit-down." I heard the phone beep and saw Emma's name finally pop up on my screen. "I've gotta go." Swiping the screen, I answered the call, "Emma?"

Her voice sounded thick, like she'd been crying, "Christopher, I'm sorry. I swear to God that I never meant for this to happen. I don't want you to worry. I'll disappear."

"No!" I shouted. "Don't disappear, baby!"

"I've got to. It's the only thing I can do now that I've messed up so badly." She broke down then, crying uncontrollably before saying, "I'm pregnant." And then she ended the call, just like that.

Time stopped. My entire body went numb.

She's pregnant?

CHPATER 22

Emma

"Who is he, Emma?" Valerie asked me as I dropped my cell on the bed and cried for the umpteenth time in the last six hours.

"I can't tell you," I whimpered.

"You can and you will." She pulled me up off the bed to make me look at her. "I know that I don't know this guy, but he sounded older to me. He's an older man, isn't he?"

I nodded. "Yeah." She could know that much.

"Okay," she let me go, and I fell right back on the bed like a limp noodle. "Since he's older, you guys might not have as big a problem as you think you do." She picked me back up. "Unless this guy is married. Is he married, Emma?"

"No!" I said, a little outraged that she'd think I'd have an affair with a married man. I fell back on the bed again as she let me go.

"You need to stop that crying and start talking, girl. Because this makes no sense to me." She sat back down on her own bed, which was only a few feet across from the one I was on. Thankfully her roommate had agreed to stay at a friend's place for the rest of the day so I could be with Val alone. "So, dry it up and start talking."

Shaking my head, I sat up but knew there was no way in the world to fix this. I wiped my nose with the back of my hand, and she made a face before throwing a handful of old napkins at me that she grabbed from her nightstand.

After blowing my nose, I said, "Look, we can't come clean about what we've been doing. I've already told you that."

"I want the whole story, and I'll decide that for myself." She crossed her arms over her chest and gave me a demanding look. "Let's start simple. What is his name?"

I wasn't planning on telling anyone his name. "No."

"Yes!" she spat at me. "And right now, Emma Hancock!"

If I wanted her help, I knew I would have to come clean, so I just went for it. "Christopher Taylor."

"See how easy that was?" She smiled at me then asked, "And why can't you two see each other in the open?"

"He's my boss. He's my father's boss. And he's my father's old college friend." I wiped my eyes with the napkins then took a deep breath. "I've really got to stop crying and start trying to figure out what I'm going to do. I can't stay here forever, that much is obvious."

"Are he and your dad friends now?" Val asked. She had a contemplative look on her, and I could only hope she was coming up with some sort of plan.

"They are." I knew it was utterly hopeless, but Val clearly hadn't come to terms with that yet. "Do you know if they still have homes for unwed mothers the way they used to in the old days?" I asked, trying to think up a plan of my own.

She shook her head. "I don't think so. Now, tell me more about this man. I can see how he wouldn't want to end his friendship with your father, but does he have any other reasons he doesn't want this getting out?"

"His daughters are pretty mean, I think. He doesn't want them to bother me, he said." I thought about what else I could do, since there probably weren't any homes for unwed mothers anymore. "Maybe I could get a job at a daycare, and that way I could learn how to take care of this baby. Then when he's born, I can keep him at the daycare with me. It's a win-win."

"Do you honestly think that working at a daycare will pay enough to put a roof over your head and raise a child, Emma?" She looked up at the ceiling as if that was the stupidest idea in the history of stupid ideas. "This man is the boss of the company you work for. That means he's got to have money, which he can use to pay you child support. So, does he have money?"

I nodded. "He's a billionaire."

Valerie gulped as her eyes went wide. "A billionaire? Are you for real?"

"I am for real. But to secure any child support from him, I'd have to tell our secret, and I can't do that." Didn't she remember how my father really was? "You do remember my dad, right? I mean, the reason we've kept this a secret is mostly because of him."

Valerie stared at me, the creases in her forehead and the way her lips pulled to one side told me she had something to say to that. "Emma, you do realize that your father will find out that you're pregnant eventually—and he won't stop until you tell him who the father is."

She's right.

"Well, I'll just have to never see my parents again, I suppose." The thought made my heart hurt. "I'm going to miss them. And I'm going to miss Christopher, too. I'm even going to miss Mrs. Kramer." And then another round of tears start up.

I'd never felt so alone in my life. All I had now was Valerie, and that just wasn't going to be enough. I fell back on the bed, putting my hands over my face as I felt the weight of responsibility for not only myself, but now a child, too.

Val took me by the shoulders and pulled me back up. "Okay, you've gotta stop doing that. It's not helping anything. Here's what I think you should do. Call the baby-daddy back and tell him he's gotta come up with something. He's a grown man; he'll figure something out. You are, for lack of a better word, immature."

"Am not!" I whined. But deep inside I knew Valerie was right.

I'd been babied by my parents my whole life, and while I'd done a lot of growing up in the last few months, I was nowhere near mature enough to raise a baby on my own. But I had absolutely no idea what to do about my predicament...

"But I can't call him and just tell him to solve all my problems. I can't put this on his shoulders. It's the woman's responsibility to make sure she's covered when it comes to birth control. I've always felt strongly about that. And I didn't even think about it for even one second. It's my fault, so I'll figure out how to deal with it. I'm sure there's a hotline I can call. I'll just go get a motel and make the call and get out of your hair."

Val didn't move. She held me there by my shoulders. "You will not do any such thing, and you're not in my hair. Look, Emma, you've kept yourself alienated your whole life. You never ask for help, even when you need it desperately. I don't know why you do that, but you've gotta stop.

And cut out that nonsense about it being the woman's responsibility—it takes two to tango, and if he didn't want a kid he should've thought about that too. You're not alone in this. There's a baby growing inside of you now. And if you don't take care of yourself, then you won't just be hurting yourself anymore, you'll be hurting him too." She pointed at my stomach. "Now, I know you don't want to hurt little junior there."

"No, I don't." I put my hand on my stomach. "I wonder if it'll be a boy or a girl? I wonder if one is easier to take care of than the other? Do you think Christopher will ever forgive me for this?"

"I'm sure he already has." Val sat on the bed next to me, wrapping her arm around my shoulders. "Give the man a call, Emma. Give him the chance to step up and do what's right. If he doesn't do what's right, then we can go from there, but you have to give him a chance. You said he's got daughters. He's a father already. I doubt he'll want this child to go through life without him."

"But I'm so embarrassed. And I'm ashamed, Val," I admitted. "I've lied for so long about where I've been going on the weekends; I'll have to explain all those lies if I came clean about everything."

"That's usually what coming clean involves, Emma—revealing all your lies." She laughed lightly. "You won't be the first or last person to get caught in a lie."

"Yeah, but I don't have to get caught in it. I can just go away and live my life without my parents. Lots of people have done that," I said.

"As if your parents wouldn't hunt your ass down, Emma." She let me go and stood up. "The reality of your situation is that you can run for now, but they will catch up to you. Your parents will find out about this baby. And one day they will find out that Christopher Taylor is that baby's father. Now you can grow up and tell them about this to their faces, or you can hide like a little kid—the kid they think you are."

She was right, and I knew that. But I couldn't ask Christopher for help. "Then I'll tell them. But I can't do it yet. I've got to let some time pass. I've got to give myself some time to accept this." I was teetering on the edge of insanity as it was; I couldn't go to my parents just yet.

Val's phone made a dinging sound, and she pulled it out of her pocket. "I've gotta go to the bathroom."

Valerie had lots of friends. I knew if I stayed around that I'd get in her way. I needed to leave. I needed to get to a motel and find a hotline so I could get the help I needed.

She meant well, I knew that. But she just didn't understand the relationship I had with my parents or my relationship with Christopher. Valerie's advice, while spot on, wouldn't work for me. I was wasting her time and energy.

Patting my tummy, I whispered, "It looks like it's just going to be you and me."

Valerie was all smiles as she came out of the bathroom. "How about a bottle of water, Emma? You should drink lots of water. I think that would be good for the baby, and you've cried so much, you're probably a little dehydrated." She went to the minifridge and pulled out a couple of bottles; walking back toward me, she held one out for me.

I took it and then unscrewed the lid. "Valerie, you're a great friend. I'm going to get going and find a motel. I want to take a long bath and just relax. I appreciate your advice, I really do, but I've got decisions to make, and I need to be on my own to make them."

She sat down on her bed. "Did you bring a bag with you?"

As I drank the water, I thought about what she'd asked and nearly choked on it. "Damn! No. I didn't bring anything, other than my purse."

She nodded. "Yeah, I thought so. How much money do you have?"

"A few thousand in the bank. I've got my bank card and my credit card with me." I thought about the cost of buying new clothes, paying for a motel, and filling my gas tank. And then I realized that I had the company car. "Damn! Damn! Damn!"

Val got up, turning her back to me. "You didn't drive your car here, did you? You brought the one the company lets you drive, didn't you?"

"Okay, Valerie. Here's what I'm going to need you to do." I put on my thinking cap. "Drive my company car back to Manchester. Go to my house and pack up everything of mine that you possibly can. You'll have to do this in the middle of the night while my parents are sleeping. I'll give you the code to the security system. Park the company car in the garage and bring my old car back here to me, then I'll have my car and my things." It was the perfect plan.

"Sure, I could do that for you, Emma." She turned back to look at me. "But what good would that really do in the long run?"

A knock sounded at the door, and she went to answer it. "I've got a much better idea."

I couldn't think of a better idea, but I was willing to hear hers. She opened the door as I got up to go wash my face.

"Emma?" a deep voice called out to me.

I didn't have to turn around to know who was at the door. And I knew things were out of my hands now.

How could she?

CHAPTER 23

Christopher

"Emma?" I watched her body freeze up at the sound of my voice. "Baby, I'm here for you." I walked into the small dorm room that belonged to her friend.

Thank God Valerie had answered my message when I arrived at Columbia. I knew Emma had to be there somewhere, but I had no idea where. Valerie had responded to my message with the number to her room, and I came straight away to get my girl back.

Emma still hadn't moved so much as a muscle. I wrapped my arms around her from behind and kissed the top of her head. It felt so good to have her back in my arms.

"You shouldn't have come," Emma whispered. "She shouldn't have told you where I was."

"I had to," her friend said as she came to stand in front of her. "I'm not letting you run, Emma. He's come here for you, and I'm not about to let you make the biggest mistake of your life by trying to do this on your own."

I had to hand it to the young lady, Valerie was an excellent friend. "Thank you for letting me up here, Valerie. After Emma called, I knew there was only one place she'd be, and that was with you."

"I'll leave you guys alone." Val looked at me with a soft smile. "It's nice to meet you, Christopher. Do right by my friend, please."

"I will, I can promise you that." I turned Emma in my arms, and she buried her face in my chest as her arms wrapped around me. "We'll lock up when we leave."

"Thank you," Valerie said just before she walked out the door. "Love you, Emma. Call me later."

Alone at last with the young woman who carried my child, I knew I had to let her know how I really felt about her. "Emma, I want you to know that I love you. I want you to know that I'm here for you and this child. And we're going to tell everyone about us now. No more hiding."

Her arms tightened around me. "I love you, too. But I'm so scared."

I'd be lying if I said I wasn't a little scared as well, but she needed me to be strong for her. "There's no reason to be afraid. You're not alone in this. You shouldn't have run off, baby. You scared me to death, you know."

She looked up at me with red-rimmed eyes. "I'm sorry. I'm sorry about everything. I should've been on birth control or made sure we used condoms, but I never even thought about it. If I'd been smarter, then this wouldn't have happened."

Swaying back and forth with her in my arms, I could do nothing else but smile into her eyes. "Don't blame yourself—I wasn't thinking about birth control either. And I'm glad this happened."

Slowly her expression transformed into disbelief. "You can't be glad about this. Don't lie, Christopher."

"I'm not lying." I pulled her along with me to sit on one of the small beds and then I pulled her onto my lap. "At first I was shocked and numb, but then it started to sink in. We're having a baby. You and I are really having a baby. And I've never been happier in my entire life." I knew my smile matched my words, and I couldn't have wiped it off my face if I tried. "I've also never loved anyone the way I love you. Having a baby is exactly the right thing for us to do, Emma. Can't you see that? This child is a product of our love. Nothing could make me happier."

Her brow furrowed, she still did not look convinced. "This isn't going to go well. This will not be easy. I have no idea how my father will react, but it won't be good at all. And I'm sure your daughters won't be jumping up and down with joy either."

"I don't care. They can all get the hell over it, baby. First of all, you won't be living at home with your parents anymore. You'll be moving in with me in my home." Watching her reaction, I wasn't exactly pleased.

Her face melted and paled. "No! Your daughters will hate me, Christopher!"

"I don't want you to worry about them. If they don't treat you right, they'll have to move out." I wasn't about to let them make Emma's life uncomfortable in the least. "I mean it. If they say one bad word to you, I want to know about it. No one, including your father, is going to say a harsh word to you, or they'll have to deal with me."

Slowly, her expression began to change. Trust began to glow in her eyes. "That's so much for you to take on."

I kissed her lips softly. "I can take it on, Emma. I want to take it on, don't worry about that. Come home with me now."

"I guess that's the best thing for me to do. We can weather this together, I think, no matter how many people will hate this." She looked into my eyes as she ran her hand over my cheek. "I do love you. And hearing you say all that stuff about us having a baby makes me so happy. I've been such a mess since I saw that stick this morning. But you're here, and you're making me feel very safe, very happy —very taken care of."

"And loved?" I asked. I wanted her to feel that most of all.

Her smile was brilliant. "And loved." She leaned up to kiss my cheek. "And I hope you feel loved too."

Turning to catch her lips, I gave her another kiss. "I do feel loved. I would've said it sooner, but for some reason it never slipped off my tongue. But now that it has, prepare yourself to hear it often."

Taking Emma out of that dorm room, I put her in her car so she could follow me home. I'd told her to call her father to let him know she was fine, and that she would see him and her mother at home the next evening to explain everything.

On my way home, I'd called my daughters and told them to meet me there because I had big news. I imagined they thought I was going to tell them that I would buy them that island they wanted. If so, they would be in for a real disappointment.

I parked my car in front of my lake house with Emma pulling up right behind me. Getting out, I hurried to reach her before she got scared and drove away. Opening the door, I took her by the hand. "Come on, baby."

"I feel like I might pass out, Christopher. I've never been more afraid of anyone's reaction in my life." She held on to me so tightly her nails dug into my arm.

"It's going to be okay. I'll take care of everything." I brought her into the home that we would now not only be sharing, but raising at least one child together in. "Don't expect any congratulations from them, but expect me to shut down anything ugly they might try to say."

"Okay, I can do this," she whispered as we went through the foyer and into the great room. "My goodness, this place is spectacular, Christopher."

"Thank you. I had the interior designed to fit my personality. I'm glad you like it." I was very proud of my home. It was the only home I'd ever considered all mine. But now, I wanted Emma to think of it as hers too. "Now that you'll be living here, we can hire the decorator to add some touches of you to our home."

"Christopher, this is all too much. I'm reeling here." She looked up at me warily.

Everything was moving too fast for her, and I could see that. "Okay, one thing at a time, baby. No problem."

She was reverting back to that shy young thing again, clinging to me like I was the only lifeline she had. I hated that she felt insecure, but I could see she was fighting it. I was proud of her for trying, and with time, I hoped to help her get back to being the secure woman she'd grown into in the last few months. The fact that our relationship had been a secret hadn't stopped her from making huge strides in her self-confidence and esteem. I hated that this pregnancy and coming clean about our love seemed to be setting her back.

The sounds of high heels clicking on the tile echoed as both my daughters came down the hallway. "Daddy?" Lauren called out. "Are you home?"

Emma's legs began to shake, and I helped her sit in a chair. I held her hand as I stood next to her. "Don't worry."

My daughters came into the great room, and both stopped in their tracks as they saw me holding Emma's hand. Ashley's mouth gaped. "Who's she?"

"And why are you holding her hand?" Lauren added.

"Take a seat, girls," I nodded toward the sofa, "and I'll tell you everything."

Lauren glared at Emma, shooting daggers with the blue eyes that looked so much like her mother's. "If you think this is going to be easy, you're wrong."

"Do not threaten her," I barked at my oldest daughter. "I won't allow that."

They took their seats with stunned expressions on both their faces. I hadn't been firm with them all that much throughout their lives. But I wouldn't let them torment Emma, and I knew I would have to be firm now.

Emma looked up at me with a weak smile. "Thank you, Christopher."

"You're welcome, baby," I said then turned my attention back to my children. "This is Emma Hancock. She and I have been in a relationship for the last couple of months."

"So, you were with her all of those weekends you were away, weren't you?" Lauren asked me. "You've been lying to us."

"If take a look at how you've been behaving, and how you're acting now, you might understand why I chose to keep our relationship from the two of you." Their attitude wore thin with me, and I jumped into the meat of the conversation. "Let me cut to the chase, girls. Emma and I are having a baby. She's moving in, and if you don't like any of this, you are free to leave our home."

Emma shook her head. "No, please don't call this our home, Christopher. This is your home and theirs. I don't want them to feel like I'm coming in and taking anything away from them."

"But you are," Lauran snapped. "You've snuck around behind our backs and gotten knocked up by my very wealthy father so you could take what's rightfully ours. Don't act innocent with me."

"Lauren, I will not let you talk to her that way." I let go of Emma's hand to walk closer to my daughters. I wanted to let them know that I would not tolerate that kind of behavior. "The fact is I'm happier with her than I've been in a very long time. And I'm happy to be having another child. If I have my way, she and I will have many more children. As many as she'll give me. Do you understand me?"

Wide eyes looked up at me with quivering lips, making me feel like some kind of a monster. Soon, tears started falling down my daughters' cheeks.

"She's fooled you. She's a gold digger," Lauren whispered. "She did this on purpose. I can see it written all over her plain face."

My hand itched and I wanted to slap my daughter so badly. I'd never hit either of them in my life, and I wouldn't ever. "I'm sorry that you feel that way. You can pack your things and leave now. I won't have Emma, the mother of my child, living in an atmosphere where she feels threatened or unwelcome."

Turning my back on my children, I joined Emma again. If they wanted to be in my future, they would have to accept the fact that Emma would be there too, and so would our child.

CHAPTER 24

Emma

The talk with Christopher's daughters had gone just about the way I had thought it would. They looked at me with hate in their brilliant blue eyes. They thought I'd gotten pregnant on purpose just to get their father's money. None of it surprised me. But it hurt, nonetheless.

Christopher took me to his bedroom afterward. He held my hand as he opened the door to the giant room. "And this is your new bedroom, Emma."

Masculinity being the central theme, the room had dark brown leathers combined with creamy fabrics that covered the furnishings. The oversized four-poster king bed had a thick coffee-colored comforter and four long fluffy pillows. "This is nice."

Pulling me inside, he closed the door behind us. "I want you to add your own touch in here, too, baby. Add some of yourself to our bedroom. You know, like you've done with our cabin in the woods. I guess we don't need to rent that anymore, now that I've got you home."

A leather sofa set in one corner looked inviting, and I went to sit down to try to figure out what I needed to say to him.

He wasn't wasting any time, trying to make me feel at home. "I'll introduce you to the part-time staff that works here. Twice a week, three maids come to clean the inside of the house. The gardeners come once a week to take care of the outside. Three times a week the cook comes in. She takes care of buying the groceries, and the maids restock the bathrooms. You really don't have to lift a finger around here if you don't want to. And if anything doesn't work for you, or makes you uncomfortable, we can change things around."

"See, that right there is the problem, Christopher. That's the way your daughters have been raised. My appearance in your life, and now our baby, threatens their lifestyle." I knew that was the main reason they didn't want to see their father with anyone, much less a fertile young woman who would conceive more heirs, cutting their inheritance down by millions.

He took a seat right next to me and intertwined his fingers with mine, holding our clasped hands on top of his leg. "They will have to get used to that fact, Emma. After all, the baby is already in existence. Nothing will change that now." He kissed my hand as he looked at me with determination in his hazel eyes.

"They will never accept me. I'm younger than they are. It's not going to be a pleasant experience, trying to be a family." I felt overwhelmed and under-experienced. "By the way, you should know that I don't have any idea of how to take care of a baby. Not a clue."

He laughed and then let my hand go to put his arm around me, pulling me close. "You can learn." He kissed the side of my head. "And we can hire a nanny, if you think that will help."

"She better be old," I said as I thought about some young woman living in our home, helping with our child.

Christopher saw right through me. "Jealous? How sweet." He kissed my cheek. "You're adorable, Emma."

"I'm also quite uneducated about pregnancy." I was as unprepared for that as I was for a baby.

"So, we'll get educated about it." He had an answer for everything. "I don't know a hell of a lot about it myself."

"I don't see how; you've had two kids," I mumbled.

"Lisa didn't let me have much to do with her when she was pregnant." He looked away as if the memory was uncomfortable. "This is going to be as new to me as it is to you, I bet. I've always wanted to be a more hands-on dad, but Lisa never let me be that to our daughters. I'm very excited, Emma. Very excited." He kissed my cheek then pulled me around until I was straddling him, sitting on his lap, facing him.

For a moment, we just looked into each other's eyes. Then I leaned in and placed my lips on his. I'd given myself to him over and over again and never made him take me. I wanted that man more than I'd ever wanted anything. And with the baby I now carried, I did feel like he was mine in almost every way imaginable.

Having this baby won't ruin anything.

Life would be very different now, though. I would live in a mansion. Drive fancy cars. Wear expensive clothing. In a year, I probably wouldn't recognize myself. And it had all started with giving myself to the man who'd stolen my heart.

The next day would be equally as brutal, as we had to tell my parents our news. But for now, we could relax and just be us. I suddenly became very excited about the future. If we could just get through the meeting with my parents, things might actually be more normal for us. No more stolen moments. No more hiding. No more sneaking. No more lies.

We had a few battles to fight. But for now, we could just make love and gather the strength to fight the next one.

Or so I thought.

Christopher's cell phone rang, and he eased his mouth away from mine. "I better see who that is." He pulled the phone out of his breast pocket and frowned at the name on the screen. "Your father. I better take this."

I climbed off his lap, feeling weird being in that position with my dad on the phone. "Remember, I'm not here."

He laughed then answered the call. "Hey, Sebastien, what's up?"

"You're one big piece of shit, that's what's up, Christopher Taylor," came my father's snarled reply.

Our eyes met, and I scooted closer to him as he asked, "What is that supposed to mean, Sebastien?"

"I got a call from your daughter Lauren," Dad said, making my heart freeze. "She told me they put two and two together when gave Emma's full name. Lauren called me to make sure I knew what was going on—I gave your kids my number when you had us over for dinner, and thank God I did! Lauren told me that you and my little girl have been seeing each other in secret for the last couple of months. She said that you got my little girl pregnant!"

"She's not a little girl, Sebastien," Christopher was quick to point out. "She's of age. And your reaction is exactly why we kept things secret." He took my hand. "We're in love."

"You make me sick," my father growled. "Send her home right now. We'll take her somewhere and deal with this pregnancy."

"The fuck you will!" Christopher snapped back. "You're not in charge of her, Sebastien."

"Neither are you," Dad shot back. "My wife and I want the chance to talk to our daughter. We want to know if you coerced her in any way. And may God help you if she tells us you have. I know Emma never would've pursued you on her own. You are one sick fucker. Do you even realize how sick you are?"

I couldn't stand it. Christopher had stood up for me, and I wasn't about to sit there and let my father speak to him that way. Grabbing the phone out of Christopher's hand, I had to let my father know I wouldn't stand for this. "Dad, you stop talking that way right now. I love him. I'm moving in with him. And we're raising our baby together."

"Emma?" Dad asked in a soft voice. "Baby girl, come home and talk to your mother and me. We can fix everything. You don't have to do anything you don't want to. But you need to know that Christopher has used you. He's too old for you, and he should've known better, but there's something wrong with him, baby girl. Come home and let me and your mom help you. We're not mad at you, honey. Only him."

"I can make my own decisions, Dad. I've *made* my own decisions. I wanted to be with Christopher from the moment I first saw him. He didn't trick me. He didn't do anything I didn't want him to do." It was never my intention to share with my father anything so personal about my sex life, but I didn't want my father thinking badly of the man I loved. "And Dad, I did make the first move. Each time, I was the one who made the advances."

"He's made you think that, Emma. It's not the truth." I hated how confident he sounded—like he would know better about anyone on this topic than I would.

"Dad, I'm not coming home. I refuse to talk to you and Mom about this if you're going to be unreasonable. I'm a grown woman. I know you don't see me that way, but in the eyes of the law, and in my own eyes, and in Christopher's eyes, I'm an adult. And as an adult, I can be with whoever I want, regardless of their age. You're going to have to get used to that if you want a place in my life and the life of your grandchild." I handed the phone back to Christopher. "Hang up the phone."

"Wait!" Dad called out.

"No," I shouted. "Christopher, please end the call."

But Christopher wasn't ready for the horrible call to end just yet.

"Sebastien, you and I should meet and talk about this. Your friendship means a lot to me, and I don't want to take your daughter away from you guys. I know you and Celeste love her more than anything." Christopher closed his eyes. "This is killing me, man. I swear I never meant to hurt you or your family."

"A fat lot of good your words do now," Dad said. "The fact is you're destroying my family, and I won't let you do it, Christopher. I will get my daughter back and I will make her see that this is a mistake. Why would she want to be with an old man? She's young with her whole life ahead of her. And you're, well, you know you're past your prime; you have no business raising a baby at your age."

I was shaking with anger at those insults. I was so mad that I couldn't speak. But my father's words were having a different effect on Christopher. He was full of guilt, remorse, and I could tell he just wanted to make things better.

"Sebastien, having you as my friend has made such a difference in my life. I regret that I've done something that's hurt you so badly. I hope that we can get past this one day. I am the father of your grandchild; that's never going to change. And I am the man who loves your daughter nearly as much as you do. I will take care of her for as long as I live—however long that might be."

Tears stung my eyes at the torment I heard in Christopher as he poured his heart out to my father. Grabbing his free hand, I brought it to my lips, and Christopher's eyes met mine. "I love you so much, Christopher. You have no idea. Nothing will get in the way of our baby and us. I promise you that."

My father wasn't done yet. "I promise you both that I will not stand for this. I will do what I have to do to save my little girl the heartache you don't seem to care about, Christopher. I'll be moving out of your house as soon as I possibly can. And I no longer wish to work for you. I'll turn in the company car in the morning."

The look on Christopher's face told me this was torture for him. "Please don't do any of that, Sebastien. Please give yourself some time. Take all the time you need. You'll have paid leave for as long as you need it. I understand this is upsetting to you and that you need time to process it all, but don't throw away your career and this opportunity."

My father didn't bother to answer, hanging up on us. Christopher and I just looked at each other.

What have I done?

CHAPTER 25

Christopher

Checking the time, I sat up, rubbing my sleep-filled eyes. The fact that Emma lay next to me making small snoring sounds filled my heart in a way nothing ever had.

She's home.

I had to wonder how things could feel so right for both of us, but not for anyone else who loved us.

It wasn't as if I'd never come up against the occasional hardhead or prejudiced type before. I'd spent decades negotiating deals with a number of characters who exhibited those exact traits. It looked liked I'd just have to step up my game with Emma's parents and my daughters. This woman and our baby were the most significant part of my life now. I had to make our families understand and accept that fact.

Getting up at five in the morning wasn't my usual routine, but I knew Sebastien was an early riser. So, I left Emma to sleep while I got up to go give Sebastien and Celeste a surprise morning visit. I might have to take one to the chin from my old friend, but if it would make him feel better, then I'd gladly take it.

Leaving a short time later, I kissed a sleeping Emma on the forehead, being careful not to wake her. If she knew what I was up to, she'd ask me not to do it, or worse, demand to come with me.

I owed Sebastien an explanation for what I'd done. He deserved that. I should've been honest with him from the start. I'd hid everything just to avoid the inevitable, but now the inevitable had to be dealt with.

Just as I pulled into the drive, Sebastien came out the door, heading to the garage. I guessed since he wasn't wearing a suit that he was about to go turn in the company car. When Celeste came out behind him, I knew that's what he was about. I'd come just in the nick of time.

Once they noticed me, they both stopped and stared at my car. Sebastien took his wife's hand as they waited for me to approach. The two looked prepared to stand their ground, and I had to admit that seeing them like that shook me a bit.

But determined to fix this for my new family, I parked and got out of my car. "Good morning." Neither said a thing. So I went on. "I want to speak to you both. I owe you an explanation for what's happened."

"You don't need to explain a thing to me, Christopher," Sebastien said sternly. "You wanted something, and you took it. Just like so many other powerful men do without a thought for the consequences. All we want is for you to do the right thing by our daughter."

"Which I intend to do," I pointed out.

Celeste shook her head. "We mean that you need to let her go."

Raising one brow, I couldn't understand how anyone would see that as the right thing to do. "Maybe we should take this inside. The neighbors don't really need to know our business, do they?" No need to create a scene for the neighbors to watch over their morning coffee.

Thankfully, Celeste concurred. "Yes, let's take this inside."

I followed them into the house, where neither saw fit to take a seat, even though that would've put us in a better position to speak more calmly. Instead of waiting to be asked to sit down, knowing neither would offer, I instigated the action. "Let's take seats and talk to each other like the adults that we are."

After I sat down, Celeste and Sebastien took places on the sofa, facing me. They were a team, and I was alone, but I didn't let that get to me, not even when Sebastien said, "You might win the first few battles, Christopher, but I assure you, my wife and I will win the war."

"You know what would be even better?" I asked. "If there were no battles and no war. All I want is for us to understand each other better. For instance, do you understand that I am the father of your first grandchild?"

Sebastien ran his hand over his brow, obviously trying to keep his anger subdued. "I don't want to talk about that right now. I want to talk about how you thought it would be okay to seduce my little girl."

How to explain this in a way that wouldn't stir his anger?

"When you met Celeste, how did you know that you were attracted to her?"

"We're not going to do this, Christopher," Sebastien told me. "We're not going to pretend that you had good intentions with Emma. Mostly because all three of us know that's just not true. You knew that she was inexperienced. I'd told you as much. That's when you decided you had to ruin her."

"That's just not true, Sebastien." Agitation began to boil up inside of me. "From the moment I saw Emma, I felt something spark inside of me. I tried and tried to not think about her, and I failed miserably each time."

"That's called obsession, Christopher," Celeste pointed out. "I think you need help. Mental help."

Looking at Christopher, I asked him, "Do you remember how you couldn't stop talking about Celeste when you first met her? Because I remember what kinds of things you did to make sure you ran into each other. I remember all the nights that you would talk about her for hours on end. You actually enrolled in one of her classes, just so you could be around her more. Does that sound like obsession too?"

"I was a kid in my early twenties back then. You're a man in your forties. Celeste and I were the same age when we met," he told me, as if I didn't already know that. "Our daughter is only twenty years old, and she was as pure as the driven snow before you came along. You've got daughters who are older than Emma. How can you justify your obsession with someone so young?"

Trying to find the words to explain the enormity of my feelings was difficult. "Emma does more than just make me happy. She's the sun in a world I hadn't realized was black. I thought I'd be fine living the rest of my life simply being alone, but content. I wasn't unhappy, just okay with how things were going. And then I saw her." I shook my head, still not fully comprehending what had come over me that day. "And everything changed. I've never experienced anything so amazing."

"And what about her?" Celeste asked. "I want to know what she felt. I'm convinced that you seduced her, Christopher. While you're a nice-looking man, you are much older than she is, and she's always been so shy. It just doesn't make sense to me. And I'm her mother—I know her better than she knows herself."

"You two have treated Emma like a child for a bit too long," I let them know as I shoved my hand through my hair with frustration. "You may think you know her better than she knows herself, but I assure you that you hardly know her at all. You know the girl you want her to be. You don't know Emma as she sees herself, as an independent, responsible woman."

The look of disgust on Sebastien's face unsettled me. "She's only twenty. You can stop talking about her age as if she's some old spinster that we've held back. Emma's always been shy and introverted. That's her normal behavior. If she's anything else with you, then you had to have pulled it out of her. She's not naturally promiscuous. It had to have been the pressure you put on her that made her give herself to you. Admit it already, so we can start fixing this shit pile you've created, man!"

"I won't admit to something that's not true." The ground felt as if it was slipping out from under me. I wasn't getting anywhere with them. "However it started doesn't really matter now. We were both deeply attracted to one another. We both acted on that attraction. And as hard as this might be for you to believe, we both thought it best to hide our relationship from everyone because of how you two and my daughters would react. And I can see that we weren't wrong to hide our relationship from all the ridicule the four of you have thrown our way."

Celeste huffed as her hands flew up. "What did you expect?" Her eyes narrowed at me. "Did you think for one second that any of us would approve of this thing? You both knew it was wrong. But the thing is, Christopher, you are an adult and Emma is a kid. Even if she's of age, you knew she wasn't mature enough to handle a relationship like this. And now you've gotten her pregnant, another thing she's not mature enough to handle. And it will be her father and I who'll end up taking care of this baby because of that."

Incensed, I said a little too loudly, "If you think you two are raising my child, you're delirious!"

Sebastien jumped up immediately. "You will not raise your voice to us, you sick son-of-a-bitch!" he shouted at me.

Celeste took him by the arm, holding him as if she was afraid he'd storm over and beat me up or something. Not that I was afraid of a physical altercation, but I didn't want to hurt him by accident. The fact I'd already hurt him emotionally didn't sit well with me.

"Let's all calm down," Celeste said, trying to de-escalate the situation. "Sit down, Sebastien. I don't want anything to get physical. We've already discussed that."

As he retook his seat, he glared at me. "You can't be there with Emma all the time. You work tons of hours each week. She'll be alone with that baby, and she'll have no idea what to do for it. It will be me and her mother who will end up being there for her and the baby, not you. You're not thinking clearly. Your head is up your ass right now—you can't see past your obsession with her. Once her pregnancy starts showing, once she has that baby and she's not the innocent little thing you lusted after in the beginning, you will lose this so-called attraction you've got for her. And you will lose interest in her."

Hearing him say such a thing rattled me. *Could I ever lose interest in the one woman who's able to touch me deeper than anyone else?*

"Christopher, please," Celeste implored me. "Do the right thing for Emma and the baby. If nothing else, you will leave her alone to raise a child she knows nothing about. And in the end, you will die long before her and your children, and she'll be even more alone then."

That thought had never occurred to me before, but it did make me think now.

CHAPTER 26

Emma

The sound of chimes woke me up out of a deep sleep. Blinking, I didn't know where I was at first. But then it all started to come together in my head. *I'm at Christopher's home in his bed. But where's he?*

I sat up, rubbing my eyes as the chimes kept on playing. Then I looked at my cell. I'd forgotten that I'd changed my ringtone the day before. My mother was the calling me.

Hoping she wanted to apologize for everything, I answered the call. "Hi." I yawned and stretched as I waited to hear her apology.

"Emma, we've just had a talk with Christopher, and he's agreed to do the right thing by you. Your father and I want you to come home now. We'll help you with everything, but you need to come home," she said.

"What do you mean Christopher has agreed to do the right thing?" I honestly had no clue what my mother was talking about; Christopher already was doing the right thing by loving me and loving our baby.

"He's letting you go," she said, as if that were a good thing for me.

"No," I simply said. "That's not what's best for any of us—not for me, him, or the baby. I'm not coming home unless he asks me to leave."

Tension filled her voice. "Don't make him go to those lengths, Emma. He's not in his right mind. Just come home. Leave before he gets there."

Now I felt as if she wasn't telling me the whole truth. "Mom, what exactly did he say to you?"

"That he was going to do the right thing," she said. "And we'd told him that the right thing would be to leave you alone. You deserve to be with someone more like you, Emma. Someone your own age. And when you're really ready for a relationship and not being forced into one the way he's done to you—"

"He hasn't forced me into anything." My stomach knotted with nausea, and I had to jump out of bed to run to the bathroom, throwing the phone on the bed as I went.

Once everything from my stomach was in the toilet, I sat on the floor, trying to catch my breath. My head hurt from the force of my heaving, and my body shook. *Being pregnant sucks.*

Once the lightheadedness wore off, my stomach growled. And just like that, I was starving to death.

There was no way in hell that I was about to go try to find the kitchen. The fact that I might run into Christopher's daughters or get lost in the mansion was the deciding factor in that.

After washing up, I threw my clothes back on and grabbed my purse, then headed out to the front where I'd left my car. As far as I knew, Christopher wasn't home. Judging by my mother's phone call, I knew he'd taken it upon himself to go see my parents without me. That he hadn't let me know his plans left me feeling a little prickly.

Just as I pulled up to a nearby fast food drive-through, my cell rang again. I'd put it into my purse, so I had to dig through it to find it. When I saw it was my father, I sent the call to voicemail. I didn't want to argue. I only wanted to get something into my stomach.

Rolling down my window, I made my order. "Two sausage biscuits and a large apple juice."

"Will that be all?" the person inside asked.

My stomach growled. "A hash brown, too."

"Drive up, please," the girl instructed me.

The breakfast was not the healthiest I'd ever eaten—and my parents definitely would not have approved of it. Not one piece of fresh fruit. Not one whole grain. Just white flour-based biscuits, fatty meat, and worst of all, a fried potato pancake. The apple juice might've passed their muster, but I just couldn't make myself care in the least.

What I did care about was Christopher and what he thought was the right thing to do. Somewhere deep inside, I knew he thought it best to keep our baby and me in his life. But a nagging fear brought on by Mom's call sat in the back of my mind. *What if they got to him?*

What if my parents had somehow convinced him that I would be better off if he left them to take care of me?

I'd never thought my parents would want to keep control over me so badly that they would consider it best to keep the father of my child out of our lives.

Driving up to the window, I smiled at the cashier as she told me the total.

Pulling a twenty out of my purse, I handed it to her. "Here you go."

She gave me the change and the bag filled with my unhealthy breakfast foods, and I drove away. The smell made me ravenous, and I had to park in the grocery store parking lot next door to dig in.

I couldn't recall ever being so hungry in my life. I scarfed it all down in record time. Then a burp came out of me that defied imagination. Gross, but I finally felt better.

Feeling more myself, I picked up my phone to call Christopher to see what was going on in his head. Before I could make the call, the phone rang and it was the man himself.

"Hello?" I asked, trying for a neutral tone; I didn't know how he'd be feeling after his chat with my parents, or if my mother had been telling me the truth. I tried to brace myself for his reply.

But no reply came. "Hello, Christopher?" I asked again. The

sound on the other end was a little scratchy, as if something was covering the mic.

Had the man butt-dialed me? Just as I was about to hang up so I could call him for real, I heard the faint sound of a woman's voice on the other end. I couldn't quite make out what she was saying, but I was soon able to make out bits of Christopher's reply.

"…you know she's pregnant…leave her…I don't care…children."

So, he was clearly talking to someone about me. But who? After the call from Mom, I didn't think he'd still be at my parents' place. I heard the woman's voice again, but couldn't make anything out of what she was saying. Did she say something about him coming back? Her voice was too far away to really tell.

But when I finally picked out Christopher's voice again, my heart stopped. "Lisa…" I couldn't make out anything more, as the rushing in my ears made me deaf to everything around me.

Shaking my head to clear my mind of the shock of hearing Christopher speak his ex-wife's name, I was finally able to make out what the woman—Lisa—was saying.

"Please…father of my children…Christopher…with me." By how clear her voice now sounded, I could only guess that she had moved closer to Christopher—close enough that his phone was now able to pick up her words as well as Christopher's.

What the hell was Christopher doing with his ex? It didn't sound like they were arguing, and from the way he had described her, he had made it clear that was the only way their conversations ever went.

But Lisa hadn't sounded angry—neither had Christopher, for that matter. She had sounded like she was trying to soothe him.

Had he gone to his ex for comfort?

And what was that bit she'd said about him being the father of her children? I couldn't help thinking that he was also the father of my child—a little, helpless baby who needed his father more than any grown daughters did. I wished I could tell that to his ex-wife, this woman whom he now seemed to be confiding in, maybe even asking for help.

"Lisa...love you," I heard Christopher reply. Without any instruction from my brain, my hand hung up the phone, and I threw it in the back seat at those words.

I couldn't have just heard Christopher tell his ex that he loves her? But that's exactly what it had sounded like.

Slumping over the steering wheel, I was so shocked I couldn't even cry. Not only was Christopher with his ex-wife, he was having a level-headed conversation with her—which he'd told me he hadn't been able to manage once in the last five years—and he was telling her he loved her?

And all this after my mom told me that Christopher had agreed to leave me.

Everything seemed to crumble before my eyes. Had I been played by an older man? Used and then left to tend to things on my own?

I didn't know what to do. If Christopher had lied to me about his relationship with his ex, and about staying with me and the baby, then he would he tell me the truth if I confronted him? And Mom had tried to make it clear that he'd already decided to leave me, and that I should go back home. The truth was that I didn't want to go home. I didn't want to let my parents take care of me and my baby. I wanted Christopher. And not just to take care of me, but to be my partner in life and the raising of our baby.

But if Mom had been telling the truth, then that wasn't going to happen now, was it?

Coming to Manchester, New Hampshire, had been the best thing to ever happen to me and the worst thing to ever happen to me. How could that be?

Nothing made sense to me. Why had Christopher come to New York to get me if he wasn't going to do what he and I had agreed was the right thing to do? Why had he told his daughters about us and our baby? He had practically kicked his daughters out of their home for my sake.

How could he have changed his mind about so much in such a short amount of time?

My head hurt with all the questions. And all I wanted was at least some closure with the man. Not a call from my mother telling me things were over between us.

As I sat in the company car, anger started to take over instead of hurt. That man owed me more than what I'd been given. He owed me an explanation. He owed me a turn to speak. And he owed our child, too.

I had to blame my parents for somehow getting into his head and telling him God knows what. But as much as I could blame them, it still hurt that Christopher had been so easily manipulated by them. And it still didn't explain why he'd gone straight to his ex after speaking with my parents. It made me think he had doubts about his love for me.

I had no doubts where he was concerned. I loved him. Even after this hellish morning, I still did.

That kind of love couldn't be shut off. And it hurt me to think that people were making him feel bad about himself for loving me. And what was worse, some of those people claimed to love me. My own parents had played a part in this.

But as the dust settled on that revelation, another thing popped up.

He'd gone to his ex-wife.

Why her, of all people?

Perhaps I didn't know Christopher as well as I'd thought. Maybe he hadn't been as honest with me as he should have been. Perhaps this whole thing had been a lie all along.

Maybe I will be better off without him.

CHAPTER 27

Christopher

Walking into my home, I let out a huge sigh of relief to finally be in my safe haven. I'd hardly had time to worry about Emma's car not being where she'd parked it the evening before—*she probably went to grab a bite to eat,* I'd told myself—when Lisa had shown up in the driveway.

The girls had obviously told her about Emma and the baby, and I suspected Emma's parents might've even spoken to her as well. I don't know why they thought she'd be able to help, but it seems they'd sent her my way as a last ditch effort to separate me and Emma. That, or Lisa had decided on her own to come over and try to mess with me one last time.

Lisa had spouted some bullshit about wanting to get back together. Even now I wasn't sure if she actually felt that way, of if she was just doing it for our daughters' sake; she had always been a great actress. She'd pleaded that it would be best for our daughters if we were back together. Why she thought I'd choose the welfare of my adult daughters, who could fend for themselves, over that of my unborn child who would need a father, I have no clue.

Wanting her to leave as quickly as possible, I'd told her in no uncertain terms that I would not be leaving Emma and our baby, and that I could never love her again. Thankfully she hadn't put up too much of a fight, likely because it was more of an act than an actual plea to get back together, and I'd watched her as she'd gotten back into her car. She'd only slammed the door a little, and with a flip of the bird to me, she'd driven off.

There was no way I was going to let my ex-wife ruin my newfound happiness. Emma and I had enough obstacles as it was without having Lisa come over and screw everything up.

Besides, the talk I'd had with Sebastien and Celeste had only served to cement my decision of what I needed to do with Emma. Now that all the unpleasantness was dealt with, today would be one hell of a great day. Or at least I hoped Emma would think so.

First, I needed to make sure my daughters clearly understood things. They'd retreated to their rooms after our conversation the night before. The fact that neither had packed up and left had led me to believe that they'd abide by my wishes where Emma was concerned, but after Lisa had shown up, I wasn't so sure. I wanted certain they hadn't told their mother to come over and that they were accepting of my desires before I went any further.

Heading into the kitchen, I found the girls eating breakfast. The cook was there, so I knew I'd catch them eating at home that morning. Their smiles put me at ease as I came in. "Good morning, you two. It's nice to see those pretty smiles on your faces this morning."

Ashley patted the seat next to hers. "Come, sit down and have breakfast with us, Daddy."

I took the seat then kissed her on the cheek. "I hope this means you two are happy for me and willing to be civil at the very least."

Lauren filled my coffee cup. "We are, Daddy. We know we were being selfish yesterday. If that girl makes you happy, then that's all that matters."

"I'm glad you feel that way." I took a sip of the coffee. "I wasn't pleased about you calling Emma's father last night. That was a battle we weren't prepared for. And I just had an unpleasant chat with your mother—I assume that was your doing as well?"

Lauren dropped her head. "Sorry, Daddy. We were just really upset and worried about you."

"There's no need to be worried about me." I pulled the silver dome off the platter in the middle of the table revealing scrambled eggs and bacon, and I helped myself. "I don't suppose either of you has seen Emma this morning?"

"No," they both said.

"Why do you ask that? Is she not here?" Ashley asked.

"Her car's gone." I shrugged. "I think she went to get something to eat. I wanted to make sure things were smoothed over with you two before I called her. Being able to deliver good news to her would make me happy."

Lauren's smile seemed a little off as she said, "If she's gone, do you think maybe she went to her parents?"

I hadn't thought that at all until she mentioned it. "Maybe I should go ahead and give her a call now."

Ashley put her hand on top of mine to stop me from getting the cell out of my pocket. "Eat first, Daddy. I don't see the need to rush anything. Unless you're worried she might not want to live here with you. At least not yet."

Lauren nodded. "Yeah. I mean, we know you two have been staying together every weekend for the last couple of months, but that's not full-time living together. It might be freaking her out some. Girls that age aren't very mature yet. She may want to live with her parents. At least for a little while. You don't want to push her, do you, Dad?"

"Of course not." But I did want to talk to her. "You guys don't know her yet. She hasn't had the easiest time living with her parents so far."

Wanting to get off the topic of Emma moving back in with her parents, I changed the subject to one I'd been hoping to talk to my daughters about for a while. "Girls, I want to introduce something new to you both."

"More new things, Dad?" Lauren asked.

"Yes." I tried to think about how to word what I wanted. "You see, most people in this world have some type of job."

"Oh, here we go again," Ashley whined.

"Dad," Lauren chimed in, "we've talked about this before."

"Well, we're talking about it again. You two need to be better role models for the newest little Taylor." I thought I'd try to get them involved with, if not even a little bit excited about, the addition to our family. "As role models, I'd like you both to find something to do. I don't care how much money you make, or even if you make any money. Volunteer for all I care. But get up each day and go do something you care about. Become responsible adults and citizens."

"That sounds boring, Dad," Lauren said. "I mean, you want us to just change around our whole schedules just to get up and get out of the house each and every day?"

"You can have weekends off," I offered. "Or whatever two days your employers give you. But for the most part, yes. I want you out there in the world doing stuff. And not just shopping or messing around. I want you both to do something that makes a difference."

The glum expressions on both their faces told me they weren't going to hurry up to find anything to do. It became apparent that I would have to come up with some ideas for them. Maybe even line things up for them.

"We'll see about it," Lauren said.

Ashley huffed. "So, does that mean that Emma has to work too?"

"Emma has a job," I let them know. "But after the baby comes, she'll have to stay home for a while to take care of it. Not that it's any of your concern. You're my children, and it's my responsibility to make sure you know what's expected out of people in life."

"And what's Emma's job?" Lauren asked.

"She's the assistant to my assistant," I answered.

My daughters looked at each other with smirks on their faces. "Oh, your employees are going to have a field day with your news, Daddy." They both laughed, and I didn't like how catty they sounded.

"Thankfully, I'm the one who signs their paychecks." I gave them a stern look. "Much like yourselves, their money comes from me. If they want to keep getting paid, they'll mind their own damn business."

Their laughter came to an abrupt stop then. "Is that what'll happen to us if we don't treat Emma the way you want us to?" Ashley asked.

I wasn't sure how to answer her. I didn't want to control my daughters with money. But then again, that was an awfully big incentive. "Don't try me and you won't have to find out."

Lauren's cell rang, and she picked it up. "Oh, it's Mom."

My heart sank as they both got up and left the room to take the call. They must've been the ones behind Lisa's sudden appearance in my driveway.

After hearing the beginnings of their conversation and getting confirmation of my fears, I contemplated following them to listen in on the rest of the call, but I'd had enough of family interference for one day. Now it was time to focus on Emma. That thought made me realize something—if Emma had gone to grab food, she should be back by now.

If my daughters and their mother were plotting against me, might they have also plotted with Emma's parents?

In a flash, I headed outside to get in my car to find Emma, figuring they must've tricked her into going to her parents' place. Pulling my cell out of my pocket, I tried not to drop it, wanting to get her on the phone as quickly as possible.

Just as I ran out the door, I saw Emma pulling up. Relieved, I ran straight to her. She parked the car and then got out, shaking her head at me. "How could you, Christopher?"

"I haven't done a thing. Listen, just get back in the car. We've got to get out of here." I grabbed her, pulling her to the passenger side where I put her back in the car before running around to get behind the wheel. "They've been plotting against us, baby."

"So, you didn't go to your ex-wife and tell her about us?" she asked.

"No way in hell." I threw the car into drive, then peeled out. "She showed up in my driveway—my daughters' idea, I now know—with some crap about wanting to reconcile. She already knew about you and the baby, and I nipped that in the bud real quick."

"And you didn't tell my parents that you were going to do the right thing by me?" she asked.

"I did tell them that." I pulled onto the road, heading into town.

Emma looked confused. "Mom said you agreed with them that the right thing to do was to leave me."

"Not in my mind, it's not," I let her know. "That's their opinion. And from what I've just seen of my daughters' and ex's behavior, it seems everyone has come up with one way or another to split us up. So, it's imperative that we stay together for the next little bit so they can't try anymore of their stupid stunts or lies. I'm not about to lose you, Emma."

"Where are we going?" she asked as I got on the interstate.

"Anywhere but here." All I wanted was to get away from everyone who was against our being together. "It's crazy to think that everyone who loves us wants to see us apart. They don't give a flying fuck about our baby and what's best for him. None of them care that we're in love. And I don't know what to do about any of it."

She nodded in agreement. "I know. I've never felt this way. I love my parents. I've believed my whole life that they only want what's best for me. Why can't they see that you're what's best for me?"

"You're what's best for me too, Emma." I slowed the car down as my heart spoke to me, telling me that now was the time to make things right.

Pulling to the side of the road, I put the car in park then got out to open the passenger side door. Emma looked at me with a smile on her pretty face. "Christopher, what are you doing?"

"This is what I meant when I told your parents I was going to do what's right." I took her seatbelt off, took both her hands, and then pulled her out of the car.

Cars zipped by us, nobody seeming to care what we were doing—and that was fine by me. The only person I needed to pay attention to me was Emma.

"This is kind of scary, Christopher," Emma said as she looked at the traffic going by us.

"Yeah, I know." I went down on one knee. "Everything about our relationship has been a bit scary. So what better way to keep that relationship growing than to add some more scary to it?"

She looked down at me, and I saw tears in her eyes. "Are you about to do what I think you are?"

"Emma, I want to marry you." I squeezed her hands. "Not because you're pregnant. I want to marry you because you're in my heart, and I know you'll be there forever. I can't imagine my life without you in it. I've loved you since the first time I saw your pretty face. So, I am asking this of you. Will you make my dreams come true and become my wife?"

Tears streamed down her cheeks as she nodded. "Yes, Christopher, I would love to become your wife."

CHAPTER 28

Emma

Running my hand over the red brick exterior of the Centennial Hotel in Concord, the place our love affair had started, I couldn't believe I had a new last name—and a husband to go with it.

Christopher held my hand as we walked into the lobby. "It seems only fitting to spend our first night as a married couple in the same room where we first made love."

"I totally agree." For once, everything felt right in the world, and that gave me a confidence I'd never had before.

No longer little Emma Hancock, being Mrs. Christopher Taylor gave me an inner strength I didn't know I had. I had a partner now for life. Someone who'd be there for me, and who I'd get to be there for, any time things got rough. Looking at the wedding ring on my left hand, I sighed and then rested my head on my husband's shoulder.

Husband!

That sounded so cool to me.

Like a whirlwind, we'd driven straight to Concord, completed the proper paperwork, and then found ourselves a justice of the peace to make our relationship legal and binding. Now our critics would have a heck of a time trying to separate us—they'd have to contend with the law now, too.

Even with all that, I knew our loved ones wouldn't take things as well as we would've liked them to. Our relationship wasn't going to be well-received by many, and we were getting used to that fact.

As we approached the desk clerk in the lobby, I got ready for the odd looks we'd get from the staff. Christopher smiled at the attendant as she greeted us.

"Hello, welcome to the Centennial. Do you have a reservation with us?"

"I made one just a short time ago. I've reserved the Governor's Suite for Mr. and Mrs. Christopher Taylor." He held up my left hand to show her my gorgeous rings. "We've just gotten married."

"Well, congratulations," she said as she smiled. I was surprised to get such a positive reaction, but pleasantly so. *Maybe not everyone will see our marriage as an oddity.*

"Thank you," I said as I smiled back at her. "We actually spent our first night together in that room. That's why we came back here for our honeymoon."

Christopher put his arm around me, then kissed my cheek. "Of course, I'm taking my wife on a real honeymoon after this."

"Of course," the clerk said. "So, let's get you newlyweds to your room then."

A few minutes later, Christopher had me in his arms, carrying me over the threshold and into the room where it had all began. "Here we are again, baby."

The bellboy put down the one bag we'd brought with us. "Congratulations, guys. You have fun now." He closed the door, leaving us alone and smiling at one another.

"I can't believe this," I whispered.

"Believe it, Mrs. Taylor." He kissed me, making my head even lighter. "I love you more than you will ever know."

Laying my head on his broad shoulder, I said, "And I love you so much, you'll never have any reason to doubt it."

On the way here, we had stopped at a department store where

Christopher bought us a couple of changes of clothing. We'd left his house with nothing but the shirts on our backs after all.

Our attire didn't speak to the wealth Christopher had. I had on a simple white dress and flats to match, and he had on jeans and a button-down shirt and sneakers. As I looked in the mirror at our reflections, I laughed.

His lips grazed up my neck as he wrapped his arms around me from behind. "What's so funny?"

"It's just that I've just married a billionaire, but we look like we bought our clothes from the discount store down the street." I ran my hand over the dress as Christopher unzipped the back of it.

He pushed the dress off my shoulders, sending it into a puddle on the floor. "We did buy clothes from a discount store down the street. But only to save time." His hands moved around my body to cup my breasts.

I covered his hands with mine. "You know what, sexy? I wouldn't care if you didn't have a dime. I would still love you just as much."

His eyes met mine in the mirror. "I know that. You've never shown me even once that you were after my money. You've always loved me for me, and that's part of what stole my heart."

As his hands moved to run over my stomach, I thought about some of the things that had made me fall in love with him. "I fell in love with the way you treated me like your equal, instead of like a kid."

Turning me to face him, his lips met mine for a second. "I've never seen you as a kid, Emma. I've only seen the inner and outer beauty you possess. I've only seen the kindness that radiates from you. And the fact you didn't see me as an old man made me love you, too."

Unbuttoning his shirt, I ran my hands all over his massive chest. "I don't know who would think of you as old, Christopher. You're in better shape than anyone I've ever laid eyes on." My mouth began to water as I touched his hard body.

With a low growl, he picked me up, taking me to the bed where he gently laid me down. I watched as he stripped away his clothes.

That spectacular body belonged to my husband. I felt as high as a kite, knowing he was mine forever.

With one hand, he ripped my bra right off me, then did the same with my panties. "I suppose I need to get a subscription to a lingerie service. At the rate you rip them off me, I'm going to need to have new bras and panties delivered weekly, sexy."

"Do that then." He ran his fingertip up my stomach then between my breasts. "Because I don't think I'll ever get tired of doing that." Getting on the bed, he pulled my legs up and bent my knees.

My entire body shuddered, knowing he was about to deliver an intimate kiss that would send me to a place only his mouth could. As his lips pressed against my swollen pearl, I closed my eyes. *I'm married to the most desirable man I've ever met.*

The thought seemed more like a dream than reality.

How did this happen?

One minute I was thinking he'd left me, then the next we were standing side-by-side saying vows I'd never dreamt of uttering.

It didn't seem real. The way his mouth moved on me didn't seem real, either. The way his hands ran over my hips and around to my butt, pulling my body up so he could devour me didn't seem real.

Everything felt so right, so incredible—so unreal.

Heaven couldn't be any better than this.

His mouth took me higher and higher until my body couldn't take any more, and it crashed, making me scream his name over and over. Soft kisses moved up my stomach as he crawled up my body.

Sinking his hard cock into my pulsing canal, he groaned. "God, you feel so damn good, it doesn't seem possible."

Moving slowly, he filled me up in a way that I knew only he could. All the doubt I'd had in the last twenty-four hours vanished as we made love. As husband and wife, we joined our bodies together in a way we never had before.

It felt so different, so permanent. And instinctively I knew we would only get closer and closer as time passed. We would build our own family. If no one in either of ours ever came around to accepting us, then so be it. We had each other and our baby, and most likely, a couple more babies before we were all said and done.

I'd never had an end goal. I'd never known what I wanted to do with my life. But now I knew. I wanted to be Christopher Taylor's wife. I wanted to raise our children together. I didn't need anything more than that. Anything else was just extra. If I never did more than that, I would still call myself successful.

Running my fingers through his thick, dark hair, I whispered, "You've made me whole, Christopher Taylor."

"Baby, you've done that for me too," he growled as he moved faster, thrusting harder. "I can't imagine being without you now."

"You'll never have to be without me." I pulled his face to mine and kissed him as he took me even harder.

Whimpering with the oncoming orgasm, I had to release his mouth as the climax hit me, and I moaned with ecstasy. "Christopher!"

His body went stiff then wet heat shot into me, his juices mixed with mine. My legs shook, and I had to put them flat on the bed. Then I realized my whole body was shaking. Only then did I realize I was crying.

He rolled off me and leaned over me, kissing my wet cheeks. "What's wrong? Did I hurt you?"

"No," I whispered. "I don't know exactly why I'm crying. I'm just happy, and kind of in shock; I don't believe this is really happening."

He ran his hands over my cheeks, then kissed my trembling lips softly. "Baby, this is all real. You and I are married. You and I are going to have a baby. And you and I will be happy from this moment on. You don't have to think about anything else. Things aren't the same as they were a few hours ago. You are my wife now. A certain amount of respect comes with being my wife. You'll see what I'm talking about when we get back home. Nothing will be the same."

His words should've calmed me down, but they didn't. "What is Mrs. Kramer going to think?"

His smile told me that was a silly thing to ask. "That our business is our business. She's not one to make judgments, baby. No need to worry about that. Do you still want to continue as her assistant? Because you don't have to if you don't want to. That's all up to you."

"I liked working with her." I thought about how hard it might be to see all the people at the company when they all knew about Christopher and me. "But don't you think it's going to be odd for us? Maybe it would be better for you if I don't go back to work there. You know, maybe people won't think badly about you if I'm not around."

"Do you think I give a shit what anyone thinks?" He kissed me again. "Besides, not everyone is going to react the way our families did. Come back to work. You'll see. No one will dare to say a word about me and you. I'm not just some guy who works there, baby. I own that company. No one from work will say a bad word against us —at least not to our faces. Now, our own families—well, that's another story, isn't it?"

With a sigh, I turned to cuddle against my husband's chest. "Let's just get some rest and deal with the aftermath when we have to and not a minute before."

"Agreed." He wrapped me in his warm embrace, and we drifted off to sleep, both of us knowing the war with our families wasn't exactly over, even if we were man and wife.

CHAPTER 29

Christopher

The entire drive back home, Emma looked worried. Nothing I said took that look off her face. So I'd stopped talking altogether.

My lake house loomed ahead in the early morning sunlight. We'd stayed one night at the hotel then decided to head back to face reality. Dealing with my daughters wasn't something I looked forward to, but it had to be done.

"Don't make them leave, Christopher," Emma said as I pulled into the garage.

"I want you to make this place your home, baby. You won't be able to do that with them around making life as miserable for you." I parked the car then we got out.

Emma clung to my arm as we walked inside. "Just promise me that you'll talk to them as nicely as you possibly can. It was never my intention to run them out of their home."

"And you're not doing that." I kissed the top of her head. "I am."

Finding the cook in the kitchen as I'd expected, she greeted us. "Good morning." Her eyes went to Emma. "I don't believe we've met. I'm Gretchen."

Emma looked up at me with wild eyes as if she had no idea what to say. So I did it for her. "This is Emma." I looked my cook straight in the eyes. "My wife."

She looked thoroughly shocked. "Your wife? When did this happen?"

"Yesterday." I ran my arm around Emma, a huge grin on my face. "And we've got more news, too. We're having a baby."

Gretchen's eyes went even wider. "Really?"

I nodded. "Really. Have my daughters come down yet?"

"They're in the breakfast nook." She smiled at Emma. "Please come and visit with me when you can. I want to get to know what kinds of things you like to eat so I can add them into the rotation. I'm very happy for you two. I have to say, I've never seen Mr. Taylor look this happy since I've come to work for him."

Finally, a smile pulled Emma's lips up, and her eyes didn't hold any fear in them. "Thank you, Gretchen. I will come to talk to you once I get settled in."

Whispering in her ear as I led her to the breakfast nook, I said, "See, I told you being my wife will be fine—some old-fashioned prudes think a different kind of respect comes with being a wife." I rolled my eyes at that, though I knew those attitudes would work in our favor.

"You were right." She laughed. "How cool."

"Yeah, how cool." I chuckled. "Now, onto the hard part: my kids."

She nodded knowingly. "Please, just try to be as kind as you can be."

"I will try." I knew my daughters wouldn't make it easy though, especially if it came to asking them to move out.

Pushing the door open, I spotted my girls as they sat at the small table. Their eyes popped as Lauren asked, "Where have you been, Daddy? We've been worried sick about you."

Ashley added, "You didn't answer any of our calls. You just disappeared on us yesterday morning."

"I overheard you two talking to your mother." I pulled out a chair and made Emma sit down in it. I could feel the tension in her body.

The last thing she wanted to do was sit down with my daughters, but we had to put ourselves in the position of authority.

Lauren looked down at the table. "You did?"

"Yes." I took a seat next to my wife. "You know, I get it. I understand why you don't want me to have anyone else in my life."

Ashley looked at me with surprise. "You do?"

"Sure." I put my arm around Emma. "You don't want things to change around here. You don't want your lives to vary one little bit. But guess what?"

"What?" Lauren asked.

"Change is inevitable." I held up Emma's left hand. "This woman is your stepmother now."

Staring at the wedding rings on Emma's finger, Lauren gasped. "No!"

"Yes," I said. "And I don't want my wife to feel like a stranger, or worse, unwelcome in her own home."

Ashley looked as if she knew what was coming next. "You want us to leave, don't you?"

Emma looked down, and I knew she felt horrible. But she would feel much worse if those two were around. "I want us all to get along," Emma mumbled.

Lauren shook her head. "There's no way, Dad. I will never accept her. Not ever."

"You don't even know Emma. And stop talking about her like she isn't here." I huffed as frustration built up inside of me. "She makes me happy. Doesn't that mean anything to you?"

"She's younger than us, Dad," Ashley said. "It's not right."

Before I could say anything, Emma lifted her head and straightened her shoulders, her newfound confidence coming back. "To your father and I, age doesn't matter," she said.

"Did you get her to sign a pre-nup?" Lauren shot back. "Because I can guarantee you that she's just after your money. She'll get it all when you die, and she knows that."

"I didn't ask her to sign anything. She's my wife, and everything I have is hers too." I decided to up my game a bit. "And if you and your sister continue to try to interfere with our relationship, then I really will cut both of you out of my will, and Emma will get it all." One more thing came to mind. I'd never threatened this before and hoped they didn't make me follow through, but I thought it might help. "Along with that, I will cut off your allowances. I'll cancel the credit cards, and you'll either have to find jobs or get your mother to pay your way through life."

Ashley looked stunned. "So what you're saying is that you're putting us out of our home, and you will take away our money unless we give you our approval on this sham of a marriage?"

"This marriage is not a sham," I let them know. "I love this woman more than I've ever loved any woman I've ever been in a relationship with. And I'm lucky enough to have her love me back. I've spent most of my life feeling nothing more than just content. With Emma, I feel alive."

"Can we have time?" Lauren asked. "Can you let us keep our allowances? We'll move in with Mom and leave you two alone. But please don't take away our money."

"Or our cars," Ashley added. "We really need our cars, too."

Emma nodded. "Please let them keep those things, Christopher." She looked at both Lauren and Ashley. "I don't want to take anything away from you two. I don't want your father to cut you out of anything. We just want to be happy, and we just want you to let us have that happiness. That's it. I don't expect you to like me. I don't expect you to like or even interact with our baby. But I do expect you to stay out of our marriage."

I had to admit that Emma surprised me. I was so proud of her—I couldn't wait to see how marriage and motherhood would help her grow even more than our relationship had. "That's all I expect too, girls. Let us live our lives, the same way I've let you two live yours."

"I don't know if I'll ever be okay with any of this," Lauren said. "But we can move out and give you your space."

"Maybe you two could meet your father for dinner once a week or something. I would hate for you to lose your relationship over this," Emma added.

Ashely looked at me. "I don't want to lose our relationship with you either, Dad. I love you. I just wish you would've found someone closer to your own age."

"And hadn't started a family with her already," Lauren added.

"Well, life doesn't always go the way everyone wants it to," I told her. "But I've got to tell you that I'm thankful that this woman came into my life, and I'm thankful for the child we're going to have. If God grants us more children, then you will have more siblings. I hope one day you will grow to love them too."

Lauren got up, looking kind of sick. "I'm going to pack. I can't deal with this. I don't know if I ever will be able to deal with this. But I'll do what you've asked. I'll give you all the space you want. But I can tell you this, Daddy, you will lose us in the process."

Ashely got up, following her older sister. She looked at me over her shoulder, and I thought she was about to say something, but she just turned around and left the room.

"That didn't go as badly as I thought it might," I said as I got up, extending my hand to Emma. "Let's get you acquainted with your home, Mrs. Taylor." I thought a guided tour would help distract her; she looked sad about my daughters leaving.

She had no idea how lucky she was that they were leaving. "I wish there was something I could say to make them stay, Christopher."

"They'll come around. I'm sure they will. They're just not used to not getting their way." Wrapping my arm around her, I kissed her cheek. "I guess before we get started on this tour that you should give your parents a call and inform them as well. I don't want them to be worried about where you are."

She'd turned her cell off, just like I had. Neither of us had wanted our wedding night spoiled by interrupting calls that would only serve to bother us. Emma pulled her cell out of the pocket of her jeans. "I guess you're right. Might as well get all the unpleasantness over with at once."

Settling in one of the living areas, I sat next to her as she made the call. "It's going to be okay, Emma. No matter what, you've got me."

With a nod, she made the call to her mother. "Hello," I heard her mother say. "Emma?"

"Yes. It's me," Emma said in a whisper. "Mom, I don't want anyone to be mad or hurt by this."

Tension filled her mother's voice. "What did you do, Emma Hancock?"

"It's not Hancock anymore, Mom." Emma looked at me as she placed her fingertips on my cheek and looked at me with loving eyes. "It's Taylor now. Christopher and I got married yesterday in Concord. I'm his wife now."

"You're his what?" she shouted. "Wife?"

Celeste sounded shocked. As if it was beyond imagination that I would actually marry Emma. I could see now that neither she nor Sebastien had any clue as to how much I loved their daughter. The thought saddened me.

"Yes, he asked me to marry him yesterday, and I accepted." Emma leaned against me as I wrapped my arm around her, holding her close. "And I've never been happier, Mom. Never in my entire life have I felt so loved and safe."

As a parent, I knew that statement had to have hurt her mother. But Celeste didn't let on that those words might have affected her. "Did he get you to sign anything before you two were married? You know, like a paper that said if you two divorce that you won't get any of his money?"

It seemed to me that everyone who loved us thought I would leave Emma destitute if we ever separated.

I took the phone from Emma to let Celeste know what I thought about that. "Celeste, I saw no need to have a prenuptial agreement with Emma. She's my wife. She's having my child. In my opinion, neither of us will ever walk away from this marriage. And if that does happen for some reason, I wouldn't send her out of my life and home with nothing. I love her. No matter what you believe, I do love her with everything I have, and that includes my money."

The way Emma snuggled up to me made my heart nearly burst with love. I adored her. Why couldn't everyone see that?

CHAPTER 30

Emma

I'd kept my job for several months after we married. Christopher had been right—the people who worked for him didn't bat an eye at our marriage. But it wasn't the people who worked there that made the place feel uncomfortable to me—it was who wasn't there. With Dad no longer working there, it just didn't feel right.

He and Mom moved back to Rhode Island, where they both took jobs at a much smaller company. I only checked in with them once a week or so. They wouldn't come around, and they never called me; I had to make the calls to them. I couldn't understand how they could be so disappointed in me over something that made me so happy.

When we learned we were having a son, I called my father to let him know. His reaction wasn't what I thought it would be. "Great, now Christopher will have a boy. He's got it all now, doesn't he?"

The conversation went no further, as he'd said he had to get back to work. I'd hung up the phone with my heart feeling like it weighed a million pounds.

As far as Christopher's daughters were concerned, they kept away from our home and their father. At times it made me mad that they were willing to keep taking his money but refused to see the man.

Christopher just kept assuring me that the day would come when all of our family members would come to realize that what they were doing was hurting them more than us. He and I were happy, whether they were pleased with us or not. We still had each other, and nothing could shake that happiness.

With no job, I stayed home and went to work setting up our son's bedroom and a playroom too. And as I worked through the decorating process, I found that I had a real knack for it. According to the interior decorator Christopher hired to help me, I had a natural instinct for colors and setting up a nice flow.

Eventually, Lawrence asked me to join his design team. I'd been thrilled, and Christopher had been so proud. I'd accepted the job, but only on the condition that I'd start after the baby turned six months old and then only part-time. I didn't want the nanny to raise our son.

We'd hired a sixty-three-year-old nanny to help us in the early stages of our son's life. The goal was having her help me learn everything I would need to know to raise a child and then we would let her go with a tidy pension to make the rest of her days a little bit easier.

Being married to Christopher was better than I could've dreamed. He made my life so much more than I ever thought it could be. It wasn't his money that made me happy, either. It was definitely the man himself.

One week when I'd been feeling particularly tired, I'd spent much of the time sleeping. He'd come in with a handful of flowers for me, waking me with a kiss. "Good evening, Mrs. Taylor."

Rubbing my eyes, I sat up on the sofa I'd fallen asleep on. "Oh, I fell asleep watching TV again. What time is it?"

"Six," he said as he wiggled the flowers in front of my face. "I stopped and picked these wildflowers for you, baby. When I saw them, I thought of you and knew I had to get some for you."

Taking them from him, I smelled them. "They smell so good, and they're so pretty." I kissed him on the cheek. "Thank you, sexy."

"Thank you," he said then scooped me up in his arms. Even though I was over eight months pregnant, he was still able to carry me around.

And people called him old? This man was in his prime.

I laughed as I wrapped my arms around him. "For what? I didn't get you anything."

"For being you." He kissed my lips softly. "For making my life so damn wonderful that I walk around whistling all the time."

"Whistling?" I'd never heard him do that.

"Yes, apparently I whistle a lot at work now." He shook his head. "I didn't even realize I was doing it until Mrs. Kramer pointed it out today. She said I seem like a new man. A very happy man."

Resting my head on his chest, I loved to hear that. "I'm so glad we found each other. Even if our families aren't."

I realized he was taking me upstairs, most likely to our bedroom. When his foot touched the first step, something strange happened. A weird cramp began in my back, and it went all the way around to the front of my body.

He felt it too as my body tensed. "Baby, are you okay?"

"I have a cramp that's kind of weird." I looked at him with confusion. "Do you think…?"

He interrupted me. "That you're in labor?"

I nodded then thought about the dream I'd been having before he woke me up. "You know what, I was just having this bizarre dream that a gorilla was coming out of nowhere and grabbing me, squeezing me."

"I bet you've been having contractions in your sleep." He carried me up to our room then laid me on the bed. Pulling out his cell, he made a note. "Okay, this contraction started at ten after six. I'll keep track of them, and we'll head to the hospital when they're ten minutes apart, the way the doctor said."

"But we're a week before the due date," I said, recalling what the doctor had told us. "She'd said that first births are usually late, not early."

"Yeah, usually. Not always," he said as he went to the closet, retrieving the bag we'd packed for the hospital. "I'll have this ready to go, just in case."

I ran my hand over my leg. "I need to shave my legs, Christopher."

He held up one finger, gesturing for me to wait as he went into the bathroom. Coming back out with a towel, shaving cream, and a razor, I saw he meant to shave my legs as I lay in bed. "Let me tend to your hairy legs, my lady."

For some reason, I found that so sweet it rendered me speechless. All I could do was smile at him as he set to work, getting my legs all smooth. And just as he'd finished, I got another weird crampy thing. "Here comes another one."

He took note of the time then looked at me with wide eyes. "They're already fifteen minutes apart, it seems. How long were you asleep?"

Thinking back, I remembered watching the first part of a movie that had started at three. "Um, about three hours I think."

"I bet you've been having contractions that whole time and slept right through them." He looked excited as he ran the towel over my legs to get rid of what was left of the shaving cream. "We're going to meet our son tonight, I'd bet money on it."

Two hours later, the contractions were coming in ten-minute intervals, and he called the doctor to let her know we were about to leave for the hospital. I took his phone from him after he ended the call. "I'm calling your daughters to tell them about this."

He looked at me with wide eyes. "I don't want them to upset you, baby. I'll call them when it's all over."

Shaking my head, I found Lauren's number and swiped it. "No, I want to let them know about this. I won't let them upset me, don't worry."

Lauren answered the phone, "Daddy?"

"No, it's Emma, Lauren." I took a deep breath to make sure my voice didn't crack, as I was beginning to fill up with emotion. "Your father and I are about to go to the hospital. The baby's coming. I just wanted you and your sister to know. You and your sister are welcome to come up there any time you want to. We'd love to have you there when your baby brother is born."

"I don't know," she whispered. "But thank you."

I'd done what I wanted and handed the phone back to Christopher. "Okay, I guess I'll let you call my father and tell him the same thing."

He nodded, then made the call from my phone. Dad answered, "Emma?"

"No, it's Christopher." He put his hand on the small of my back, steering me to the door that led to the garage. "Emma and I are on the way to the hospital. The baby is coming. We wanted you and Celeste to know that you're welcome to join us for the birth or to come whenever you want to."

Dad didn't say anything. He'd hung up the phone. I saw that as a sign that he didn't want to know any details about the birth of his first grandchild. That hurt.

But on the ride to the hospital, Christopher had raised my spirits again, making me laugh as he made funny breathing noises while helping me through the contractions, which had quickly gone from ten minutes apart to five.

Not long after getting into the hospital bed and hooked up to all kinds of things, the contractions began to get stronger and closer together. And I started to get irritable with the pain. "When can I have the epidural?"

The nurse who'd just come on shift looked at me like I was crazy. "You wanted an epidural? No one told me that. We can get you one right away."

"For the love of God!" I squeezed Christopher's hand as another bolt of pain took my breath away.

She took off to get someone to do the epidural, and I moaned with the pain. "Breathe, baby. Come on," Christopher coached.

I couldn't do it though. It hurt to breathe. Thankfully a doctor arrived not much later and gave me the epidural, and in no time at all

I was cool as a cucumber. The hour was midnight when my parents walked into the room.

To say I was surprised just didn't cut it. "Mom! Dad!"

Christopher smiled and hurried to shake Dad's hand then hug Mom. "I'm so happy you two came!"

Mom came to me, hugging me. "Of course we came. This is our grandchild. How're you doing, baby girl?"

"Fine now." I ran my hand through hair that Christopher had lovingly brushed for me. "Now that I've got the epidural. I gave them hell up until then."

"That she did," Christopher agreed.

Mom sat down on the long window seat as Dad came to me. He placed his hand on top of mine. "You look pretty good for a girl in labor."

"Thanks," I said, trying hard not to cry. Seeing them there meant the world to me, even though I'd tried to ignore my disappointment when I thought they wouldn't be there.

The nurse came to check me, pulling the curtain around me to give us a little privacy in the room. Christopher stayed right by my side. "I'm getting the doctor. It's time to start pushing this boy out," she told us.

My eyes went to Christopher. "You ready?"

He nodded. "You?"

"Sure, why not." I'd just wished that his daughters would've come, but I didn't say anything.

Right behind the doctor, two blonde heads came into the room. Christopher couldn't believe it. "Lauren? Ashley? You came!"

The girls hugged their father, and I started crying, I was so overwhelmed. Lauren looked at me with concern. "If we're making you upset, we'll leave, Emma."

I found that very nice of her to say, and it made me cry a little harder. "No! No, I'm so happy you guys came." I looked around the room at our families, who finally seemed to have gotten it through their heads that we really did love each other—and them, too. "I'm so happy all of you came. This means more to me than you will ever know. To bring little Colin into this world with his entire family around is a dream come true—I never thought it would happen."

Christopher agreed. "Yes, it is a remarkable feeling, having you all here to welcome Colin to our family." His hazel eyes glistened as he looked at them all.

And then my heart erupted as my parents and his daughters gathered around my husband, hugging him. "You guys!" I wailed. "I love you all so much!"

Thirty minutes later, Colin was born. He was quickly passed around to his sisters and grandparents, and then his father before being nestled in my arms again. Our little bundle of joy had brought us all back together.

We finally had our happily-ever-after ending. But really, it was just the start of a happy beginning.

The End

Did you like this book? Then you'll LOVE Dirty News: A Bad Boy Billionaire Romance (Dirty Network Book 1)

A new television network was looking for newscasters, an opportunity of a lifetime.
But when the boss told me the new morning news anchor would either be me, or the most beautiful woman I'd ever seen, he messed up my world.
She was smart, funny, and sexy as hell.
Only problem was the rules the boss put on us.
If you work for WOLF, you cannot have any physical relations with your coworkers.
Our heat couldn't be denied—rules or not—we had to have each other.

Her body bent to my will, letting me take her higher than she'd ever been. And she did the same for me. Forgetting each other for the sake of the job wasn't going to work for us.

So where would that leave us?

Start reading Dirty News NOW!

ABOUT THE AUTHOR

Mrs. Love writes about smart, sexy women and the hot alpha billionaires who love them. She has found her own happily ever after with her dream husband and adorable 6 and 2 year old kids. Currently, Michelle is hard at work on the next book in the series, and trying to stay off the Internet.
"Thank you for supporting an indie author. Anything you can do, whether it be writing a review, or even simply telling a fellow reader that you enjoyed this. Thanks

©Copyright 2021 by Michelle Love - All rights Reserved
In no way is it legal to reproduce, duplicate, or transmit any part of this document in either electronic means or in printed format. Recording of this publication is strictly prohibited and any storage of this document is not allowed unless with written permission from the publisher. All rights are reserved.
Respective authors own all copyrights not held by the publisher.

Created with Vellum

Lightning Source UK Ltd.
Milton Keynes UK
UKHW052318211022
410900UK00003B/85